EM1LY LE1GH
CURTIS

JOD I'S
STORY

 FriesenPress

One Printers Way
Altona, MB R0G 0B0
Canada

www.friesenpress.com

ISBN
978-1-03-916365-2 (Hardcover)
978-1-03-916364-5 (Paperback)
978-1-03-916366-9 (eBook)

1. *FICTION, CONTEMPORARY WOMEN*

Distributed to the trade by The Ingram Book Company

Dedicated to my husband and my beautiful boys. You pulled me from the dark and will forever be my light.

"She is a beautiful piece of broken pottery put back together by her own hands. A critical world judges her cracks while missing the beauty of how she made herself whole again."

—JmStorm

PROLOGUE

She looked at the baby struggling to breathe. It was a boy. His eyes were swollen shut, and his small chubby body was slippery and pink. She placed him against her chest and felt the glowing warmth of his skin against hers; their hearts beating as one. She breathed in the scent of him and kissed his chubby cheeks. He began to cry, and she held him closer, not wanting him to be heard from above. The special moment shared between them was quickly extinguished as cold, steely fear crept in. This was no life for a child. The only thing she could offer her baby was an escape, something which she had never been able to offer herself. She knew what she needed to do to save this child from the evil that would inevitably come. Time was against her. She held the baby tightly to her chest, kissed his forehead and cheeks once more before placing her hand over his mouth and nose. She cried as she felt him struggling against her for air.

She panicked when she heard the slam of a car door followed by the thud of his heavy work boots on the kitchen floor. She heard the sliding of the dead bolt, and his footsteps

headed down to the basement. The last thing she saw as the light went out of her eyes was his smile as he lifted his son in his arms.

CHAPTER 1

1991

Jodi drew in a sharp breath at the sight of herself in the filmy gas station mirror. A fresh bruise was beginning to show under her left eye, the latest gift from one of her nightly suitors. The dim lighting did nothing to soften her reflection. Once upon a time, she had been beautiful, but now she could barely recognize the person staring back at her. Her once youthful face was long gone, surrendered to the ravaging effects of the drugs. Her dark hair used to shine with lustrousness, but now it was thin and limp, and could barely hold a braid. Her camisole was tinged yellow from days-old sweat and hung loosely from her bony frame.

She turned on the faucet and tried in vain to rinse the taste of another old man's filth from her mouth. She drank long and hard from the sink, and the acrid, rust-colored water immediately made her stomach clench and tighten. Jodi hastened towards the stall, grimacing in disgust. As she sat, she stared at the walls, which were crudely decorated with toilet poetry, swastikas, and numerous numbers to call for

a good time. She took it all in; there was everything from epithets of hate to declarations of love. The floor was wet and littered with damp toilet paper and Lord only knows what else.

"How did I end up like this?" she asked herself. She knew, but it was better to be ignorant than pick the scabs of old wounds.

Once she finished, she washed her hands and splashed water on her face, then looked into her tattered bag. She changed into a semi-clean t-shirt and sprayed herself with cheap dollar-store perfume. She ran a brush through her greasy hair, trying her best to make herself look present-able. It took her forever to painstakingly apply her best face. Make-up can do magical things for at least a few hours. Concealer was able to hide most of her scabs and bruising.

It turned out that she liked to pick at her skin when she was high. Unbeknownst to her, she would itch and scratch, pick and poke until puss spilled out and a crater formed. Jodi hadn't even known she was doing it in her euphoric state, but her body did not lie. She applied blush and bronzer to add color to her washed-out face and accentuate her sunken cheekbones. She then worked with her eye shadow and mascara to smoke her deep brown eyes and added a pretty lipstick to plump her full lips. Lastly, she carefully penciled and shaded her eyebrows. Jodi looked at herself again and breathed deeply. To the passing onlooker, she almost looked as though life hadn't kicked her one time too many.

She rinsed her mouth again with a small bottle of Listerine and used her finger to scrub her teeth before shooting the

small bit of dope she had left, temporarily quelling the itch inside her. It was all she had anymore to mask her pain. This time, when she looked at herself again, she tried a smile. She could almost see herself in there, a faint glimmer but still there. She grabbed her bag and headed out.

Jodi walked up and down the same filthy street all day, watching and waiting. The quiet hunger of want and need steadily replaced all thoughts of anything else. She looked up and watched in breathless anticipation, her heart quickening a beat, as a discarded cigarette fell from the scaffold to the ground below. She moved towards it immediately, sending a quick prayer that it wouldn't land in a puddle or become crushed under foot. She got to it just in time and took a deep drag, letting the soothing burn of the nicotine quiet her hungry lungs. The butt was surprisingly dry, a welcome change. She had started to become accustomed to feeling the moistness from a stranger's lips glossing hers in a slick of revulsion. Unfortunately, it was not unappetizing enough to decline the offering.

She savoured each and every puff, taking her time, feeling her lungs expand with the smoke and her bloodstream pulse with the high of the nicotine. She hadn't had a cigarette in at least twenty-four hours. She held her breath until it pained her, then released the smoke contentedly in a large plume. Now that the pangs of one addiction had been restored to a

dull throb, she became increasingly aware of the other angry lion beginning to awaken inside her. She needed to score. It seemed she was always hungry for something to fill the deep hole inside her. No matter what she threw into that bottomless pit, it continued to grow and fester. She was able to push it all down and lose herself in a cloud of relief when she was high, but unfortunately, this lacked permanence. She felt the tips of her fingers start to burn and reluctantly threw the last of the cigarette away.

It was still too early to start work so Jodi sat with her back against the wall, cup in hand, in her usual spot. She watched as the people on the busy street walked past her without so much as a glance—ignoring her very existence. She knew she was invisible to them, insignificant and of no value. If they did look at her, it was seldom with kindness, but rather straight-up disgust. She hoped she would be just visible enough to someone today to be able to make enough money for a warm drink and something to eat.

A little girl skipped towards her, full of exuberance, happiness, and life. She had big, beautiful eyes and a cherubic smile on her little cupid-bow lips.

"Hi there, miss! What's your name? I am Annabelle! I am going to the zoo today!" she blurted out in one quick, excited sentence.

Little Annabelle was still innocent enough that all she saw

when she looked at Jodi was a nice lady she wanted to talk to. Jodi looked to her mother, who reeked of superiority disguised as class. The mother had pretty hair, pretty clothes, and an expensive purse. The only thing that she lacked in her perfect persona was compassion. Jodi could see unbridled distaste in her barely withheld sneer as she pulled her daughter clear of her, inserting a distance between them and her that would always exist.

Jodi listened to the harsh whispers between the mother and daughter as the space between them and Jodi widened.

"Annabelle! She barked. Get away from her! We do not talk to people like that."

Little Annabelle looked back at Jodi with a confused look on her face, the lights in her eyes changing. Just like that, another innocent child had been tainted, the ignorance and hate spreading unaltered from one generation to the next.

Sometimes, a more compassionate mother would stop and hand her child a dollar. The child would bound then towards Jodi and place the money in her cup, giving her the brightest smile. The mother would smile as well, and they would hold hands and walk away with the feel-goods, but Jodi knew that—at the end of the block—there would still be the accompanying explanation. Although more polite and well-intentioned, the rhetoric would end the same, though in a softer tone.

The more Jodi really thought about it, the more she felt the anger and rage burn inside her—a red-hot boil that threatened to bubble over. There was no reason to blow the

lid off the pot though; it would not change anything. She had no choice but to deal with it. Nothing good would come of her unleashing her anger, other than reinforcing society's already low opinion of her.

It frustrated her to no end. Although she was human, just like them, she was unable to express human emotions to the world without being judged. If she were to be seen by society as happy, they would assume she was in good spirits and not in need.

If she were to express anger, she would be deemed volatile and dangerous. The unanimous conclusion being that she was strung out on drugs and out of her mind, of course, an object to veer quickly away from. A phone call to the police was most often the solution to the problem posed to them.

Expressions of sadness were ignored and considered to be another manipulative tactic. Jodi's face was devoid of any emotion. There was nothing left to hope for. Her face was one of indifference after years of defeat and acceptance of her situation, but of course, that showed them only that she really didn't care and was doing nothing but looking for hand-outs. It was a hard pill to swallow, but she had no other choice but to choke it down. She'd be left with the awful, bitter aftertaste, one that she could not flush from her mouth even if she had water to drink.

As she sat there, day after day, hungry, begging for food, and recovering from last night's rape, people would occasionally stop and ask her to explain to them why she could not just get a job and live decently.

Get a job!? How do you propose I do that? How do you propose any of us do that?? 'Oh, you work on the street? No address, no identifying documents, no resume, or experience, just got out of prison or have a criminal record?' No one hires people like that! People like me! How can I even begin to dig myself out of the hole that society *has buried me in!? People like me are lost in the cracks of a broken system! And people like you—people who could have intervened and saved me—dropped the damn ball! So, how do you think I got here?!*

They would lord over her, dangling their money like a carrot, waiting to see if she could tell them a story worthy of their charity. Jodi would simply tell them that it didn't work like that, if she answered at all. She knew that she'd never be able to quickly wrap her story up into a neat-enough package. *Could anyone?* Even if she could somehow manage to explain, she knew that they would never acknowledge the pain she had endured or admit even a small amount of culpability for how she'd ended up where she was. She knew that those people asking the questions were the same people who had helped to create her situation by stealing her culture, identity, language, and family. Or at least, they were cut from the same cloth.

They were often the same people who would exploit her to fulfill their own sick fantasies. They paid for people like her; they kept her in business. *How could I make any money selling sex if they weren't paying me for it?* To them, she was nothing but a dirty little secret, existing only to be played with for their pleasure. Once the deed was finished, she would be

left with a few crumpled bills and a black eye. The "respected businessman" would drive back home, set down his briefcase in the porch, and greet his wife with flowers and a kiss.

She was hated by others because no "upstanding citizen" would ever admit that, in the dark of night, they needed what their wives would never give them. They needed to let that twisted seed—carefully concealed deep inside them—sprout. They would never be able to get away with their depravity in real life without going to jail. She was their creative outlet. They had paid for her, and she was now their property. Consent had been bought and assumed to cover all bases—boundaries of any sort was a foreign concept to them. Once she was in their car, she would accept whatever they dished out, by will or force.

Jodi sighed in despair as she waited for a Good Samaritan to walk by. The shelter had been closed for two days straight now, and she was starving. The buck fifty in her cup would buy her no more than a chocolate bar. If she was unable to gather any more, once again, she would be forced to choose food over water.

At dusk, she got ready to begin the night. She strolled down to her side of the strip to meet up with the other ladies of the night. As always, they would check in with each other, laughing hysterically as they shared their funniest escapades of the week. She loved these women. They were her tribe.

Women who truly understood her and with whom she shared common ground.

Jodi turned the corner, a little surprised not to have already heard the usual merriment of their voices carrying through the otherwise quiet night. It was extremely odd. Everyone was usually out at this time of night. She scanned as far as she could down the street and saw that they were indeed there. The girls were all huddled together in a tight circle. She began to feel a palpable heaviness in the air. The girls were so absorbed in their discussion that they were not even jumping into the waiting cars.

As she got closer, she saw that most of them were crying, while others were pensive and trying hard not to let their tightly bottled emotions escape. Overall, the message she received from their body language was that something bad had happened to one of them.

"What's going on? Is everything okay?" Jodi asked as she approached them.

They all looked at her, sadness etched on their faces.

"It's Katie," Crystal said. "She's...." Unable to finish her sentence, she pulled Jodi into their circle and held her close as another round of fresh tears started.

Word on the street was that Katie, who had been missing for the past few days, had been found murdered in the early hours of the morning. Her body had been dumped in a ditch outside city limits, so bloodied and battered that they'd had to identify her with fingerprints. The cops had come by asking about her, but of course, wouldn't tell them why they were

asking or what had happened. Someone on the street—a police informant—had finally passed the grisly details down through the grapevine.

Fear ripped through Jodi, raising all the hair on her body as she listened to the graphic details of the damage that had been inflicted on Katie's beautiful little body.

Of all the people this could have happened to, why Katie?

Katie was young and vibrant. She was new at the game and a touch ditzy but endearing and sweet as well. The best word to describe her was "spunky." Still naïve about what her new occupation entailed; she would speak about her life as if she were Julia Roberts awaiting her Richard Geer. No one had wanted to burst her bubble. It was better to just let her enjoy her happiness while it lasted. They knew that the light would disappear from her eyes soon enough, and the colours would wash from her face. Her youthful beauty and personality would become rough, and she would start looking as hard as the rest of them.

When Jodi first saw Katie, she thought she looked like she should be twirling around on roller skates under a disco ball. It was an impression that never faded. She always wore bright pink, blue, or green eyeshadow, and you never saw her without a cherry lollipop in her mouth. She wore her hair in pigtails, adorned with neon-coloured scrunchies and brightly covered barrettes. She loved fluffy, pink, white, or baby-blue sweaters, which she would pair with sparkling miniskirts. Her neon stockings came in almost every colour of the rainbow. The one constant of her ensembles were her

pink stilettos, which fastened on both sides with cute little bows. The girls all loved those shoes, and they had loved her. Katie had quickly won the hearts of all of the old battle axes on the strip—quite the triumph as a rookie.

There definitely was an established pecking order, and new girls usually had to fight and claw for even a small piece of territory. But not Katie. Even before she had skipped down the street with her lollipop, they had loved her. Not only was she their favourite but she was also quite popular with the pedophiles and perverts that strolled the strip. She looked like a ten-year-old girl, and the streets were full of people who liked that. Because she was so young, innocent, and full of life, they had all worried about her constantly. Now, it appeared, they'd had every right to worry.

They were all terribly shaken by Katie's death, and there was a lot of tension on the street that night. Whoever had done this to her was still out there somewhere, hunting, and still in their area. As for Katie, they knew that no one would ever come to claim her body, and she would be buried alone in an unmarked grave.

Sadly, thought Jodi, *she will be forgotten in a month.*

Jodi knew that there was no lesson to be learned from Katie's death, and that it would not deter any of them from doing what they did. They all knew the risks. If it weren't murder, something else would surely put them in the ground. One way or another. *Besides, it is not like we have any another choice. We must work to survive ... even if working is what ends up getting us killed.* She wished she were amused by the irony.

Most of them were comforted by the thought that things like what happened to Katie only happened to "other people" and were able to assume that it would never happen to them.

Several weeks later, things on the street had returned to normal. The wave of fear that had rippled through their community had calmed down, and everyone had moved on with their lives. The girls met up again on the same corner and followed the same routine as always: laughing, chatting, bitching, and cat-calling the male sex workers on the other side of the street.

The weather was still nice, but there was a bite of cold in the air, a warning of what was to come. It was that time of year when Jodi would savour the last touches of warm fall weather. She knew that, very soon, she'd be freezing her ass off in the dead of winter. Soon, they would all have to lean on each other for support, sharing what little they had. It was not unusual for the girls to pool their nightly earnings together over the winter months, when business all but crawled to a halt, doing so meant another day above ground.

Jodi took her time getting to work. She was tired and wanted nothing more than to rest somewhere warm. She could not afford to take the night off and so resigned herself to the chill and trudged slowly through the neighbourhood, looking into the windows of people who lived a beautiful life and had beautiful things. Lost in a fantasy world of dreams

that would never come true, she realized that she'd walked a little off course and wasn't quite sure where she was. She stopped and turned around in a circle, trying to get her bearings. Directly behind her was a large church, with a steeple, a bell, and a stained-glass Jesus. Her jaw clenched at the sight of it. She stared at it for a long time, hatred burning her cheeks red.

Church, she thought with an ugly, sneering expression that would have startled her friends on the street, *where the "holy" congregate ... living the way God intended. Well, you can clean the outside of a glass, but the inside is still dirty.*

The church was cruel. The church was poison. No one holy would ever admit that, of course. She had *chosen* to stray from the path. *The same path I was never allowed to walk.* Despite what the bible says—judge not and love all—she had never been anything but judged, excluded, shunned, and oppressed. Unwelcome. In the eyes of the church, she had always been a sinner, born into savagery and wildness, with a skin colour they did not like for no reason other than that they simply didn't.

No matter what they did to her though, and no matter how extreme the punishment had been for refusing to convert—to conform to their concept of God—she would never believe in their god. *Why would I? What has their god ever done for me?*

She had experienced firsthand how the church callously and unapologetically ripped babies and children from their "unfit" mothers' arms, sentencing the bereft mothers to never ending heart break. The discarded offspring were shipped

off to residential schools or foster homes to be emotionally, physically, and sexually abused.

Even those children "lucky" enough to be adopted to white middle-class parents were deprived of their culture and made submissive, resigned to the fact that they did not, and would not, ever truly belong anywhere.

Jodi closed her eyes and tried to calm her breathing. In the darkness all she could see were the ghosts of hundreds of Indigenous children crying. When the shells of their souls were discovered, the church feigned shock and concern, all the while refusing to admit culpability for the irreparable damage, they have done ... fighting in court to avoid providing the victims and their families with compensation. The church's apology was akin to putting lipstick on a pig and might as well have remained unsaid for all that it was worth.

The church had broken her.

Old wounds bled as Jodi made her way back towards the strip, but she managed to stem the flow as she joined the others mentally preparing herself for the night ahead. She watched as—one by one—the girls climbed into cars, trucks, and mini vans—some of which were falling apart and others so luxurious it made your heart hurt. The luxury cars usually belonged to society's elite, those who could never even fathom the destitute of the women they picked up. They had so much money that there was no way they could spend it, even with their thousand-dollar bottles of wine and seven-hundred-dollar socks. The amount of money they collectively wasted on the frivolous could feed the entire country without even

denting their bursting bank accounts.

One thing that Jodi still found surprising was just how many politicians blazed their campaign trail through the strip. They would pick up several women at once, for elite-members-only parties. Bring your own money, cigars, and whiskey, and we will bring the women.

The voters had no idea what their representatives did in their spare time. When they weren't stepping up to podiums and promising to clean up the streets and rid the city of the "vermin who have taken up shop," they were spending tax payer's money to take the same "vermin" to their men's getaway retreats, often leaving them with illegitimate children they could not afford but were condemned to abort. The whole thing disgusted her and made no sense.

How am I the villain in this story?

Jodi, no stranger to waiting her turn, stepped impatiently from one foot to the other. The transsexual people were always the first to go. Lucrative, extraordinarily successful men were the first to condemn these beautiful people, lobbying to pass bills to prevent their basic human rights. Funnily enough, however, in the dark of night, the transsexual people were the most sought-after gems upon which to act out their dirty fantasies before going home to their professional strait-laced lives.

Next were the young ones—the younger they were (or looked) the better. There was no shortage of pedophiles trying to prevent jail time by paying for their perversion. Next to go were the woman who provided or fell into the

category of one-off fetishes. Men liked to check things off their sexual bucket lists. The next to be chosen were the minorities—mostly picked by men who preached hate and white power in their daily lives but had no issues dipping into colour in their off time.

Still, even the seediest John had standards, and woman like Jodi were about the lowest you could go, even for those illegally exchanging money for sex. Jodi had been in this game a long time and had learned exactly where she stood in the pecking order. She was often the very last choice.

Although she was young, and skilled in her occupation, her body bore the damage of the hard life she led, giving her a stereotypically strung-out look: extremely underweight, sunken eyes and cheeks, limp greasy hair, and a face and body full of red scabs. There had been many times in the past few months where Jodi had had no choice but to trade sex with the less fortunate men on the street for food, drinks, smokes, or drugs. The amount of money she was able to earn by selling her body dwindled more as each year passed, and she knew that it would soon dry up completely.

All the veterans of her profession would soon start to die off, from overdose, suicide, disease, or murder. Those who managed to keep breathing would soon have nothing left to offer and be replaced by fresh meat. That was just how it worked.

CHAPTER 2

1 9 6 5

When Frank had been small, he'd lived alone with his father in a small, rough-looking house in the thick of the woods. Although he had no memory of her, he knew he must have had a mother once, though his only proof of that was his own existence, and the fact that, in his anger, his father would often tell him he was a *'cunt just like his bitch mother.'* He had never even known her name, always sensing that the topic was off limits and never asking about her. Sometimes at night though, he would imagine her. In his fantasies, she was pretty and would flit around in the house, making him pancakes for breakfast, and singing him to sleep at night.

The house he was brought up in was nothing short of a nightmare—the stuff of horror movies that no one would ever believe. For as long as he could remember, his father would come into his room every night, repeatedly stripping him of any dignity he might have attempted to cultivate. He spent his childhood serving his father and paying dearly for any mistakes he made. He was punched, choked, burned,

starved, and sodomized. That was his existence until eventually, as a teenager, he'd run away and lived on the streets.

He grew up quick and hard out there, picked up over and over by the police for petty crimes. Each time he was arrested, he would be sent to a new juvenile-detention centre, all of which were run by ex-criminals and pedophiles. The boys in their care were never rehabilitated but treated as commodities to be farmed out to different "work sites." Time after time, he would escape from one facility only to be picked up and sent to another. Every time he got free, some sort of sick internal pull would drag him back to his father and all the horror that went along with him.

Frank's life had drastically improved after his father was found dead in his room, a bullet to the head. They ruled the cause of death suicide, but Frank knew better. He had a quiet house to himself and had almost given up committing crimes altogether. There had been a small but healthy insurance policy left to him by his father, and he would busy himself during the days fixing up the neglected house. He had even looked into a carpenter apprenticeship and thought maybe he could live an honest life.

But just as he was settling into a groove, with a promising future on the horizon, he was picked up on a sexual-assault charge. Unfortunately, he was old enough now to be tried as an adult, and he did some serious time in prison. Any thoughts of living an honest life were long gone by the time he got out, hardened, hateful, and ready to unleash his fury on the world.

Even as he had served his time, he had started to fantasize ...

to plan. He knew exactly what he would do, and exactly how, and he honestly believed that he had earned it. After years of holding back, he was finally going to get what he wanted.

Frank approached his old, dilapidated house. The years had not been kind to it, leaving it forgotten and decrepit. All the lights were out. The town had long considered it abandoned, though Frank found that this was not so. In his years of absence, an old man had taken up residence, sharing what was left of Frank's house with his two snarling dogs.

Old, rusted cars and junk littered the property. The yard was carpeted with rotting leaves, the flagstones were cracked, and the steps to the house sagged heavily and were crumbled and broken in places. The windows were cracked and several of the shutters were askew. *Home sweet home*, Frank thought, smiling humourlessly.

Frank had been scoping out the house at a distance for months. Like clockwork, every night at ten p.m., the old man would let his dogs out the door. In the evening, he would turn on a dim exterior light and sit on the crumbling porch, chain-smoking cigarettes and drinking from a small flask until he nodded off. After tiring from chasing each other around the yard, the dogs would bound up what was left of the stairs and jump up on the old man's lap startling him awake. Once he realizes where he was, he would pet his dogs, and then retire for the night. At eleven p.m., the small

flicker of light barely visible in the top window of the house would go out. And then all would be quiet until seven a.m.

Tonight, was the night. Frank watched as the dogs bounded out of the house, and the old man sat down in his chair. He then opened his satchel and pulled out a container. He had made the dogs a special treat for their last meals. Frank threw the large balls of hamburger meat, generously spiced with rat poison, over the fence to the left side of the house, out of sight of the old man. The dogs' noses immediately caught the scent of the bloodied meat. They ran to the side of the house, both dogs reaching the first ball at the same time and going for it. The larger dog growled and snapped at the smaller dog, showing his dominance, and the smaller dog skulked away, watching as the bigger dog lay down to enjoy his feast.

Now Frank was worried. He had not thought of this. If the larger dog ate both balls, he would still have to tangle with the smaller one. He was ready for option two, but it would ruin the "surprise" element of his plan. As deep in the woods as they were, he knew that firing the weapon he had concealed in his coat might still bring attention from town, which was the last thing he needed. Not to mention the shotgun that always leaned against the wall beside the old man on the porch. While he doubted it was a real threat, it wasn't a risk he was eager to take.

Once the larger dog settled into his meal, the smaller dog finally picked up the scent of the second ball. He rushed over to it, trying to gulp it down as fast as he could, but his actions had caught the larger dog's attention. A scuffle quickly

ensued, with the larger dog the winner once again, gobbling down whatever scraps had been left. Frank prayed that both dogs had eaten enough.

He looked over to the porch and saw that the old man had nodded off. The dogs, contentedly full now, sniffed around the yard, looking for more treats. It did not take too long for the poison to circulate through their bloodstreams. Frank watched them as they tried to retch but were unable to bring anything up. They whimpered as they fell, and then rocked back and forth, trying to get back up. Soon, they were on their sides and foaming from their mouths, struggling to breathe. Eventually, they both started to seize. It didn't take long from that point for their hearts to stop. He watched as the larger dog took its last breath, the smaller dog following him minutes after.

Frank smiled to himself and checked back on the old man, who was still snoring softly. Time for phase two of his plan. He walked around to the back of the fence where he had noticed that the chain link had rolled up from the ground. Crouching down and then lying on the dead grass, he slipped one arm and his head into the opening, taking his time. It was a tight fit. At one point, as he crawled through on his belly, he got stuck and started to panic, but he was determined, and finally managed to squeeze all the way through, suffering a few scratches as the metal of the fence raked his back.

Inside the yard now, Frank climbed back to his feet and crept quietly around the house until he found himself on the porch, standing directly in front of the old man. He pulled

out the black garbage bag from his pocket and stepped closer, looming over him now.

As if sensing his presence, the old man startled awake, confused, and trying to get his bearings, trying hard to understand what was going on. Frank took advantage of this moment and pulled the plastic bag tight over his head. The old man struggled, kicking his feet, and flailing his arms. He tried to scream, but the plastic only filled his mouth.

Frank had never strangled someone before, and it caught him by surprise how long it took. His hands and arms started to ache as he pulled the plastic bag even tighter and waited for the old man to give up the fight. After what seemed like a long time, the old man pissed himself and his limbs slowly stopped moving. Frank continued to hold the bag tight over his head for another five minutes until there was no doubt that he was dead. The old man's body was lifeless, his chest no longer trying to rise up and down.

Frank looked at his watch. Overall, it had taken almost twelve minutes. He was not a fan of this killing method.

He grabbed the old man by the feet then and pulled him down the stairs. It would have been easier to lift and carry the old bag of bones, but there was no way he wanted the old man's piss and shit all over him.

It was a long back-breaking night. When he was finished, Frank unceremoniously kicked the old man's body into the makeshift grave, his beloved beasts following him in quick succession. As he was filling the hole back in, a large bird suddenly swooped down at him from above, and Frank swung

the shovel at it, frantically thrashing the air and trying to protect his head.

As a boy, he had once seen a bird plucking the eyes out of a dead cat on the road and he still dreamt about the gruesome scene. He had been horrified but also curious as he'd stood over the cat. He had disassociated then, locking himself safely inside that imaginary place he often visited, only coming back to reality when the bird had begun to attack him to get back to its meal. He had been badly scratched and had run home crying, but he had found little sympathy there. Ever since that day, he had hated birds with a passion.

This one settled itself by the grave now and stared him dead in the eyes, nothing behind its gaze but cold malice. Frank could hardly breathe. Finally, it took flight, soaring towards him one last time—sending him falling backwards to the hard ground—before disappearing into the darkness of the sky.

The bird had unnerved him badly and stolen the excitement of his special night. After taking a minute to calm down and pull himself together, he finished filling in the hole, then entered his old home. Making his way down to the basement, he stood for a long silent moment, looking around. It was perfect. The time had almost come for Frank to put his plan into action. The bird was long forgotten. It was time to start the renovations. He had a lot of work to do to get things ready.

Frank had first seen her *riding* her bike down the road to the playground, little streamers hanging from her handlebars,

CHAPTER 3

1 9 9 1

Sheldon waited until his father passed out drunk in his chair before quietly slipping out the back door of the cellar to start his long walk through the woods and into town. It would take more than an hour, but he didn't mind. The forest was quiet and peaceful, and by the time he got there, the town would be too. No one was ever awake at this time of night, and he could walk, clear his mind, and just be with himself.

When he finally arrived in town, he headed right for the shoreline, climbing down the wooden steps and inhaling the smell of fresh water and sand. The sound of the waves ebbed and flowed like a lullaby. He watched as they crashed against the rocks, sending cold spray up into the night air. This was his favourite place, and his only escape from Father.

The sound of a guitar playing awoke Sheldon rudely from his reverie. He looked over to the right, towards the sound, and saw a small gathering of people sitting around a campfire up ahead, laughing and singing and getting louder and louder. The merriment in their voices could only be attributed to the

alcohol he assumed was sloshing around in their red solo cups.

His desire for peace and quiet now ruined, Sheldon stood up and brushed the sand from his jeans. He turned up the collar on his coat to keep out the chill of the night air, stuffed his hands in his pockets, and set out for the long walk home. As he crested the top of the stairs, he heard a car door slam and quickly looked up. That is when he saw her: the most beautiful girl he had ever seen.

"Where are you headed, handsome?" she asked him.

Sheldon tried to stammer out an answer and could feel his face redden. She laughed and flicked her fiery-red, waist-length from her face and back behind her shoulder.

"How about you stay here with me?" she said.

Sheldon had never had any friends. Even through his school years, he had just blended unnoticed into the background. He glanced back down towards the beach seeing once more the jovial group entertaining themselves around the fire and felt both anxious and uncomfortable at the thought of joining them. He knew that he did not belong here.

His elusiveness had piqued Penny's curiosity. She could sense his shyness and reveled in it. He was the perfect plaything. He would put her up on a pedestal and bathe her in complete adoration, even as she kept a heavy foot on his head. She smiled at the thought. Her ego could use a boost after last night's fight with Chad and their subsequent breakup. This guy was decently attractive and would be the perfect tool to make Chad jealous.

"What's your name," she asked with smiling eyes.

"Sheldon," he said, shyly, looking nervously at the fire again. "My name is Sheldon."

"It's okay, handsome," she said. "You're with me. My name's Penny, and you'll be my date for the night."

Sheldon was torn between his painful social awkwardness and his desire to be close to her. Luckily, there was no decision for him to make. Penny put her small warm hand in his and pulled him back down the stairs and towards the fire.

After introductions to people that he didn't know, with names that he wouldn't remember, Penny settled next to him on one of logs around the fire and placed a red solo cup in his hands. Sheldon smelled its contents, and his eyes watered as the strong alcohol hit them. She watched this play out and nodded to him to drink up. Sheldon took a deep breath and swallowed the drink down. It burned and tasted like gasoline and for a minute, it took his breath away. He choked and sputtered. Penny giggled at him, and he smiled as the warmth of the alcohol bloomed in his stomach. Relaxation, which he had truly never experienced before, coursed through his bloodstream, flushing his cheeks.

"First time?" Penny asked.

Sheldon grinned at her sheepishly, knowing that she most definitely knew the answer. The look in her eyes and her coy smile also suggested that she wasn't just referring to the alcohol.

Penny put her hand in her pocket and pulled out a cigarette. Sheldon watched as her face was briefly illuminated by the glow of the lighter. The soft orange light on her face was more

than enough to stop his heart dead in his chest. She met his eyes as she took a large drag and then passed the cigarette to him. Penny laughed at him again as he tried to take a puff and once again coughed and choked.

"I guess tonight is a night of firsts?" She giggled. "Here, I'll show you how," she said. "First, you breathe in like this," she demonstrated, inhaling softly.

Sheldon watched her breasts rise and pull tight against her sweater. The light from the fire made her eyes come alive and the gloss on her lips sparkle.

"Then," she said, "you gasp ... like you would if your mom walked in on you jerking off."

Sheldon's face flushed at her analogy.

Penny laughed then—either at her own comment or his expression—and asked, "Do you like to jerk off?" She burst into giggles as she saw him blush an even deeper shade of red.

Sheldon took the cigarette from her and tried again, tasting her bubble gum lip gloss on the butt. This time, he managed to inhale without choking and only a bit of coughing.

"Better," she said, with a glint in her eyes.

Penny nestled into his arms then and lay her head on his chest. He put his arms around her shoulders and held her tight. She had been right; it was a night of "firsts" because in that moment, Sheldon felt his heart flutter for the first time. As he looked across the fire, his body thrumming with this new-found feeling, Sheldon noticed a guy staring at him intently from the other side, his brows furrowed. Blond and burly, this guy obviously wanted Penny in his own arms. He

did not, particularly care. He was too overwhelmed with the feel of her body against him to worry about anything but staying in that moment for as long as it was possible.

At the end of the night, a little tipsy, Sheldon walked Penny to her car, where she turned and pressed her back against the driver-side door. Holding her hands, Sheldon stared deep into her eyes. Penny pulled him into her then and placed her lips on his, her soft tongue flitting in and out of his mouth. She smelled of vanilla and tasted of bubble gum. An electric feeling coursed through his body, his heart pounded, and his cheeks burned.

After a long moment that was not long enough, Penny pulled away and looked at him, asking, "Same time tomorrow?"

"Most definitely," he replied.

Sheldon stood back and shoved his hands into the pockets of his coat, as Penny opened the car door and climbed in. Giving him a bright smile, she started the car, reversed out of the spot, and drove away with a little toot of her horn.

Sheldon rocked back on the heels of his feet as he watched her go. *That was unbelievable!*

He headed towards the road to begin his long walk home. Just then, with the roar of a revving engine, the burly blond guy with the angry eyebrows pulled up beside him in his truck, sneered at him, gave him the finger, and then peeled out of the parking lot spraying gravel and dust behind him.

Sheldon did not let it bother him for long. As he walked home that night, he felt like he was floating on a cloud. He

could still feel her tongue in his mouth, and the butterflies and electricity were still flip-flopping in his stomach. As he lay in bed that night, he barely remembered the walk home, thinking only of her and basking in this glorious feeling.

CHAPTER 4

It was beyond the time where someone would be wanting sex. It was a work night, and the bars had long closed. Jodi was about to leave when she finally lucked out. A beat-up old car slowed, trolling its way down the strip. Spotting her, the driver pulled up to the curb and rolled down the passenger-side window, motioning for her to get in. She climbed in next to him and took in the familiar smell of cheap aftershave and cigarettes.

Jodi looked over at him and felt relieved. He was older, with grey-white hair. You could tell he had once been fit, but over the years, he had started to fill out. He looked sad. She speculated that his wife had passed recently, or else he was a bachelor who lived at home. Perhaps, he was just lonely and yearning for comfort. Sometimes men like this even just wanted companionship and to be held.

"Hi, darling, what can I do for you?" Jodi asked.

"Sex," he whispered.

"The going rate is thirty dollars an hour. That okay?"

He nodded but still had not made eye contact with her.

This was normal. Older gentlemen were often embarrassed and unsure of themselves in this situation. He seemed incredibly nervous. It likely hadn't been his first troll down the strip. He had probably tried several times before but had been overwhelmed with the feeling of shame, a feeling she was well accustomed to. His body language confirmed to her that he was most definitely having some sort of internal struggle, second guessing his decision. Jodi guessed that he had not been able to sleep tonight and had taken a drive to clear his mind, the need for consolation hitting him hard when he'd seen her all alone, prompting the snap decision to pull over and let her in ... that it was now or never.

He pulled away from the curb and headed outside city limits. Soon, they were parked far away from prying eyes on a back road shrouded in the secrecy of darkness. They had complete privacy now, and she could feel his nervous energy building up. This was it. The anticipated act would now begin. He stared straight ahead, hands clenched so tight on the steering wheel that his knuckles were white. She heard his breath quickening and could see beads of sweat appearing on his forehead.

"It's okay, darling," she said soothingly. "Don't be scared. We'll take it slow and can stop at any time if you aren't comfortable."

He placed his hands on either side of his head then, leaning forward and pressing his forehead to the steering wheel. She momentarily thought he might cry, and she started to reach over to comfort him. Before her hand touched him though,

he sat back up, took a deep resolved breath, and reclined his seat back.

There we go, she thought in relief. He was finally ready to let go and let the process happen. Jodi turned her body towards him and gently trailed her fingers down his thigh. His body stiffened.

"Relax, honey," she said. "It will be just fine."

Jodi leaned over and began to unbuckle his belt and unzip his jeans. She heard the uptake in the rhythm of his breathing. His body was still tightly clenched, and she could tell that he was extremely nervous and starting to get agitated that his sex was failing him.

It would take longer than she had expected to make him comfortable. That was perfectly fine by her. Jodi would much prefer spending her time with a lonely man in the warmth of his car, to being tied to a bed and sodomized without mercy. She enjoyed the feeling of safety and the protection from the elements that the car offered her. The autumn nights were cold. She really did not have anywhere to go anyway. If she were lucky, he would drive her to his place after and let her spend the night to absorb as much comfort as he needed from her. Although rare, this had happened to her before, the relationship lasting a few days. Jodi would relish the comfort of a real bed, hot water, and warm food—even a few new outfits to make her look presentable in public. Inevitably though, the drugs would call to her. The John would find her strung out or realize that she had stolen money or valuables from him, and back on the street she would go.

After several minutes of fondling, the man still was not aroused. She would need to try a different approach. She moved her head down towards his lap. This did the trick. Jodi felt his hand grab her hair, pulling and releasing with the rhythm of her movements. He began to rock his pelvis back and forth, grabbing her hair again and guiding her mouth up and down. After years in this business, she had learned that men often did this unknowingly, so overcome with arousal that they could not help but push up and down on a woman's head to increase their pleasure.

He motioned for her to stop, and Jodi sat back, unbuttoning her shirt before wiggling her pants down and taking them off. He laid his seat all the way back now and pulled her towards him. Crawling over the console and straddling him, Jodi put her hands in his hair, letting him control the rhythm of her hips. His hand reached up to her throat then, gently rubbing her neck and shoulders. Of course, she had never found any sexual pleasure from these encounters but did her job dutifully, making sure she feigned pleasure to increase his enjoyment.

As she waited for him to finish, she watched the windows slowly fogging up behind them, which was her favourite pastime in these situations. Her eyes wandered from one window to the next, down across the seat. She caught sight of a cherry red lollipop stuck to the floor, covered in hair. Her eyes focused sharply then, and she spotted a flash of pink peeking out from under a rumpled blanket; the spike of a pink stiletto with a tiny bow fastened to the side. Her heart

lurched and started to race as the puzzle pieces slammed suddenly together. She froze involuntarily, no longer moving to the rhythm the man had set. Cold, icy terror filled her stomach, and her last thought was that this was finally it: the end of the misery. *Another spot on the strip will be empty tomorrow night. Free for the taking.*

Her sounds of pleasure had abruptly stopped, and he felt her body tense. He looked at her then, her eyes were staring straight in front of her, full of terror. *Probably saw bubble-gum bitch's shoe.* His sexual excitement exploded as he tightly grabbed her throat and slammed her head off the driver-side window. *Too bad for her...* He clamped down tighter and tighter on her throat, slowly cutting off her oxygen.

Just as she was on the verge of blacking out, he would loosen his grip slightly, allowing her to breathe again, though not letting go. He looked at her, as he lowered his head and began to viciously bite her breasts, sinking his teeth deep into the delicate skin, tearing it. He looked at her as his mouth dripped blood, his eyes jet black and wild. There was no humanity in them now, nothing but pure carnal enjoyment. It was clear that he was well practised in his pursuit of these pleasures.

Jodi, stunned, was in agony from her wounds and fully under his control, when he punched her in the face. The last thing she felt were bones shattering before everything went black.

Jodi awoke in complete darkness, waves of pain coursing through her entire body. With every bump that jostled her, the pain in her head and face became more excruciating. Pain the likes of which she had never felt before—so bad that she could almost ignore the agony in other parts of her. She tried extremely hard to ignore it. To not think about it. Her eyes still had not adjusted to the darkness, and she had no idea where she was. She lifted her arms painfully and attempted to try to map out her surroundings, only to find that she was completely closed in on all sides.

She felt vibrations running through her body then, and though her ears were ringing loudly, she was suddenly aware of the rumblings of an engine and the crunch of tires on pavement. She realized that she was in the trunk of a moving car, and panic quickly ensued as claustrophobia set in. All at once, she remembered the events of the evening and started to hyperventilate, knowing that her ordeal had not even started yet. Many a working girl had been in this situation, though few lived to tell the tale. The incomprehensible horror of their stories was now hers, playing out moment by moment, the ending likely grim. There was no escape, and she realized that she had no choice but to surrender to the situation.

The car came to an abrupt stop. A moment later, the trunk opened. She squinted and raised her hand to her eyes to block out the light. She could tell by her attacker's hungry

eyes that her night had only just begun. She did her best to brace herself for the pain that would surely erupt when he pulled her from the car. She could only pray that this was where he killed her, and that it would be quick, but in her heart, she knew she would not be so lucky.

He pulled her from the trunk by one arm and a leg and dumped her on the cold, hard ground, stones grinding into her already screaming body. He put his hands under her armpits to hoist her up to her feet, but when he released her, she fell flat on her face, her legs numb from her confinement. As she rolled to her back, she felt a fresh spurt of blood burst from her nose and pour over her lips, the metallic taste of it fresh in her mouth now. She just wanted to sleep, but every time unconsciousness tried to take her, pain would jolt her awake.

With a grunt of effort, he rolled her back onto her stomach. Then she heard the sound of tape being ripped from the roll and felt the stickiness of it as he wound it tightly around her wrists behind her back. She had nothing left in her to even struggle as he opened the rear car door, yanked her up, and threw her face down on the back seat of the car.

She wanted to raise herself up but could not with her arms trapped behind her. Her broken, battered face pressed into the worn-out material of the backseat, making it harder and harder to breathe.

He was pissed off. In his excitement, he had taken things too far and too fast, and now the girl was nothing but dead weight. He was not free to manipulate her as he pleased,

and she would almost certainly die before he could get all he needed from her. He fed off terror and powerlessness. This one was just lying there like a dead fish, not nearly enough to fulfill his sadistic lust and need for total control. Reaching into the back seat, he slapped her as hard as he could ... staining her body with angry red handprints. Her body barely responded, barely a whimper escaping the bitch's mouth. Even so, as he stared at her bloodied body, he felt his arousal stir.

Jodi had been unconsciousness for a long time now. Though she had started to resurface more than once, she would quickly fall back into the abyss ... into nowhere ... where she was no one ... and felt nothing.

The last time she had started to wake up, she heard her mother's comforting voice, far away and barely audible, gently whispering her back to the safety of oblivion:

"Sleep now ... my beautiful baby bird."

CHAPTER 5

Sheldon returned to the beach every night that week, waiting for Penny. He would wait for hours, and she would never show. He didn't have her phone number or her address, so he had no choice but to wait for her to come back for him. He was getting increasingly disappointed as each night became a repeat of the last. He tried to be open minded and positive, focusing only on the possibilities that would not break his heart. *She said next week, not tomorrow night.* This was the one he liked best and felt was the most logical. It gave him hope. *I just misheard her.*

Then again, maybe she had been busy at school and had simply forgotten, or there had been a death in the family. If she had had to leave the area suddenly, there was no way she could have notified him.

There were a few other options that he shuddered even thinking about: her getting injured or sick, in an accident, or (worst-case scenario) dead. He tried to avoid those thoughts. Always though, nudging him in the back of his mind, was the thought that she had stood him up. That she had woken up

that morning hungover and full of regret; or her memory had been foggy, and she had only slightly recalled the evening. He tried to push this as far down inside of himself as he could. He could not bear the idea that this was even a possibility. Their connection had been genuine, their spark intense.

On Friday night, he made his way down to the beach again. He was almost ready to descend the stairs when he saw her car pull into the parking lot up ahead of him. Waves of relief washed over him, and his heart filled once again. She had not seen him yet. So excited was he that it took all his energy not to sprint towards her and call her name. He just kept walking and smiling as he watched her pop the trunk and lift out a large picnic basket and blanket. His heart skipped a beat. She had planned a romantic evening for them. He could not wait to lay her down on a blanket and kiss her.

As he got closer, he saw the passenger door open. The large burly blond guy from the previous week lumbered out of the car. Penny may not have seen Sheldon, but it was clear that her date most certainly had. Taking the basket from Penny's hands, he closed the trunk and picked her up, seating her on the trunk of the car. She giggled as they kissed long and passionately. She wrapped her legs around his waist and sighed as he kissed her neck.

"Chad!" she said as she pulled away, breathless. "At least wait until we get to the beach!" She jumped off the hood of the car, and they walked hand in hand to the steps. Chad looked directly at Sheldon, smiled at him, and gave him the finger.

Sheldon stood there frozen, his heart shattering.

"Hey, Sheldon!" Chad said with a smirk. "Fancy meeting you here."

Penny looked over, saw him there, and gasped. "Oh, Sheldon! I am so sorry! I did not mean for this to happen. It just did and ... I am so sorry." She stood there with what looked like genuine pain and regret on her face. She even tried to go to him, but Chad grabbed her arm, pulling her back and redirecting her towards the stairs. Sheldon watched as they argued. Penny looked at him, guilt painting her face. He watched as she struggled with what to do. He saw her hesitate, and then watched as she followed Chad down to the beach.

Completely numb to everything, Sheldon must have sat there for hours. Before Penny, he had never known a single moment of love, or even tenderness. When it had come, he had soaked into the feeling, basking in its warmth. It had given him hope that a better life was waiting for him. But that candle had been snuffed out hard, its wax too low for the wick to ever light again.

He did not remember getting to his feet, beginning the walk home, or making his way through the deeper parts of the forest trail, but when he finally looked up, he realized that he was only about ten minutes from home, walking along the side of the narrow dirt road that cut through a wide clearing nearby. Headlights were coming towards him, and a horn was blaring. Startled and a bit confused, he pushed even further off to the side. Looking around and trying to process the driver's reasoning, he saw that a medium-sized

dog was standing in the middle of the road, frozen in the headlights, and that the car was driving too fast to stop. It hit the dog, throwing it up over the hood, and without so much as slowing down, it continued toward town.

Penny temporarily forgotten; Sheldon ran to the side of the road. The dog was still alive but would not be for long. He held it in his arms and stroked its soft fur. Within minutes, it had taken his last breath. Sheldon picked up the lifeless body, held it tight, and kissed its warm head. Then he carried it home and around to the back, where he dug a small grave for it. When the hole was deep enough, he lovingly placed the dog into its final resting place, covered it gently with dirt, and then filled the rest back in. Physically tired and emotionally exhausted, he knelt beside the grave for a long time. With no gas left in the tank he crumpled in a heap and faded into a restless sleep.

1 9 7 6

Sheldon always hated Christmas—or dreaded it at least. It always brought to mind the worst day of his life.

Santa never came to their house for Christmas. He once asked Father why Santa had visited all the kids in his class but never stopped at their house.

"The last time he tried to come here," Father had growled, "I shot six of his reindeers and told that fucker if he ever came here again, I would blow his head off!"

That night, Sheldon had written a note to Santa and told him that he understood why he never came to their house, that he was sorry about the reindeers, and that he hoped they were feeling better. He had never mentioned the topic with his father again.

Still, he always looked forward to the school Christmas party on the last day of school before the holidays. It was exciting! Everyone brought in cookies and treats. To be polite, he would not take any, as he had nothing to contribute, but at the end of the day, his teacher would always give him a big napkin full of treats to take home. Every year, in elementary school, his teachers would always ask him to stay after class once the party was over. On top of the baked treats, they would give him a small little box with an orange, chocolates, a pair of gloves, and a hat. He never knew why they did this every year, but they always did. They would also give him pencils and paper and crayons. One year, he was even given new winter boots and snow pants. He always left these clothes and school supplies at school in his locker though, so Father would not destroy them.

He would wait all night until Father was asleep in his chair and then hide the oranges, cookies, and chocolates in the secret hiding place in the back of his closet. He loved when Father locked him in the closet for punishment. He would carefully take the little yellow blanket that smelled of pretty flowers out of its hiding spot in the very back of the closet, where he had found it when he was small and wrap himself in the soft knitted fabric. In the days and weeks that followed, one punishment at a time, he would eat a small piece of chocolate or section of orange. He would savour every bite and ration the treats so they would last as long as possible.

One Christmas morning, he heard rustling downstairs when he woke up. He slowly crept down the steps, hoping that it was Santa. Maybe he had risked coming because Father had been gone all week. He was immediately disappointed when he realized that Father was back, fast asleep in his chair. He loved when Father left him alone, and sometimes he wished he would never come back. The rustling continued, followed by whimpering. He noticed that there was a cardboard box by Father's chair. He tiptoed towards the box and realized the sounds were coming from inside it. He did not dare open the box, knowing it could be a trap. He sat on the carpet far outside of Father's reach and just examined it, trying to figure out what could be in there.

Father snored for what felt like hours. When he finally woke with a snort, Sheldon braced himself for his morning beating, putting his hands up to protect himself. Surprisingly, after a few minutes, he still had not been kicked. He slowly squinted his eyes open, still leery and anticipating punishment. Finally, he

met Father's eyes. There was no coldness in them today, and he began to relax. Sometimes Father would get like this and would play a board game with him or take him to get an ice cream. He cherished these moments, when for just a moment, he saw goodness in his father. Sometimes he would even ruffle the hair on his head.

Father gently kicked the box towards him and was actually smiling—not the sick smile, but the warm one.

"Open it," he said.

It even seemed like Father was happy and excited to see his reaction. Sheldon opened the box, still slightly afraid, and looked down to see what was making the noises he had heard. He saw a small brown and white puppy with long ears down to his feet and droopy-looking eyes. The puppy looked up and started to wag her tail and turn around excitedly in circles. Sheldon immediately fell in love. He fell hard. He could not believe that Father had gotten him a puppy. It was a Christmas miracle.

"One of Okie's bitches had a litter of pups. I took him to the cleaners, and he had no money left to put on the table, so he gave me this pup to bet a few more hands. This is a pure-bred basset hound. The bitch is registered with the Kennel Club and everything. Okie was able to hang on for a bit longer, but in the end, I took all his money and his dog."

Father laughed at his own good fortune. "There's food, and a bed for it in the kitchen, and here.... I got you something else." He pulled out a small chocolate Santa and grapes from the bag beside him. Sheldon jumped up and down with happiness. He could not believe his luck! Father had changed, and they were

going to start having fun together! In his excitement, he went to hug Father, and was scared for a moment when he felt his body stiffen and tense, but in a few seconds, Father loosened just a bit and patted his head.

"Go take that dog outside before it shits on the floor," Father said then, trying to regain his tough image.

Sheldon picked up the small puppy, cradled her in his arms, and laughed while she wiggled, licking his face, and wagging her tail. He could not remember ever feeling this happy. He named her Shelby. His teachers were so happy for him when he told them he had gotten a puppy for Christmas, and all the kids surrounded him, asking questions about her. It was a bit odd though, because when he looked at his music teacher, her lips were pursed, and she had a worried look on her face.

He began to understand that look as the days went on. No matter how many times he took the puppy out, she would keep peeing on the floor. He tried his best to clean up the mess before Father saw it. The first time his father had seen pee on the kitchen floor, he had grabbed the pup and ground her nose hard, back, and forth, in her own piss. Shelby had screeched, and Sheldon was terrorized watching it. Shelby had whimpered for hours afterwards. He had taken her outside in the shed and pet her, but she kept crying and was not able to walk or move.

As much as he wanted Shelby in the house, he knew it was best to leave her outside in the shed, so she did not have any accidents in the house and was far away from Father. He set up her bed and a bunch of blankets in the shed to try and keep her warm. In the morning, Shelby's water was frozen, and he had to beat

the bowl on the ground to break it up and then refill it. He held her tightly in the blanket and breathed his hot breath on her to warm her up. Shelby never stopped shivering. She never licked him anymore or wagged her tail. The next morning, he came out to find Shelby frozen to the ground in the shed not moving.

Sheldon screamed in horror. He ran into the kitchen and carried hot water to the shed, pouring it over her to melt the ice under her, praying that if he warmed her up, she would be okay. After the ice melted, he held Shelby in his arms and realized that she was never going to wake up. He screamed then, loud, and long. Father came outside when he heard the commotion.

"Well, Sheldon, clearly you cannot even take care of a puppy, you fucking idiot. You are such a dumb useless fuck!" he said, as he kicked him to the ground.

Father took the pup from him. Sheldon laid on the ground for so long that he had gotten frost bite on his toes, hands, and ears. Days later, the tissues blistered and wept, and all the skin slowly peeled off. He never cried in front of Father, but every night, he cried himself to sleep.

1991

Sheldon could feel the cold burning in his body as he lay on the ground. His sadness was replaced by anger, and it grew and grew until it bubbled over into a red-hot rage. He got up off the ground and stormed into the house. He heard the *Price is Right* blaring on the TV, and from behind Father's chair, he could see the back of his head. He crept slowly and carefully towards Father, and as he rounded the front of the chair, he saw that he had passed out again. Beer cans, empty chip bags, and ashtrays overflowing with cigarette butts decorated the living room. Father's hand was hanging down where it had fallen when he'd passed out, and between his nicotine-stained fingers was a cigarette that had burnt itself out.

The air in the house was stale, reeking of dirty ashtrays, Dingy sweat soaked the ribs of Father's white tank top. He was in his underwear, one hand still inside the elastic band. He had passed out scratching his balls. Sheldon took in the scattered chicken bones on the carpet and saw the shiny glistening of chicken grease coating Father's chin and neck, as well as several pieces of fried skin resting on his shirt. The nails on his fingers were long and yellowed, the beds of the nails full of dirt and grime.

Sheldon shifted his eyes to the gun rack on the wall. He walked over and slowly picked up one of the rifles. He put

the rifle to his shoulder and fingered the trigger. The rifle fit perfectly into the nook of his shoulder as though it had been made for him. He stared through the scope, slowly adjusting it so that the front of Father's head was in perfect range. He had been doing this every night now for the past two years. He felt powerful and confident with the rifle cradled into his shoulder. He was finally in control, and one sudden pull of the trigger would splatter Father's brain all over the wall. He slowly depressed the trigger and waited in breathless anticipation to hear the satisfying sound of the click. This was where he would always stop, never having the courage to pull the trigger. He put the rifle back on the rack and grabbed the keys to the car. On his way out the door, he prayed that Father would never wake up.

CHAPTER 6

Jodi awoke to the sound of tires screeching to a halt and a woman screaming.

"Oh my god! Oh, my fucking god! Christ, John! Look at all that blood! Is she even alive?" The woman was near hysterics.

"Yes, she's still breathing, Martha. Get the blankets from the trunk."

Jodi felt waves of excruciating pain course through her body as she was picked up and laid down on the back seat of a car. Her head throbbed and felt like it would snap right off her neck.

"John, look at all this blood!" Martha said, her voice trembling. "Who on God's green Earth would do such a thing to another person?! God, drive faster! She is fading fast." Panic was clear in the woman's voice.

Somewhere in between the fringes of unconsciousness and barley conscious, she was taken back to a memory of long ago, when she was a little girl. She had gone swimming in a lake near where they were living. The water was not as warm as she had thought it would be, and it was not too long after

that when she had jumped out, frozen and shivering. She had not brought anything to dry herself with or huddle into to keep warm. It was a hot, clear sunny day, and she could feel the sun warming her skin. She decided she would lie down on one of the big flat rocks on her tummy and warm up. She felt warm and cozy, and it wasn't long before she was lulled to sleep. She awoke to her mother shaking her. "Get up, child. Get up." She looked up sleepily and saw her mother's face, wrought with worry.

She had spent the next two weeks in bed. Her skin was horribly burnt, and it bubbled and blistered. The feel of the fabric moving over her skin sent fresh waves of pain through her body. She was itchy but could not scratch, and despite the heat of her burnt skin, she was frozen. She laid like this for days, with Mother giving her water and applying a strong-smelling salve to her front and back every few hours.

Her body felt like it was on fire, an itch so deep it was too much too bear. She could not stop her compulsion to scratch and kept scratching harder and harder—hard enough that she started to scream.

She shook herself violently from the dream, her body burning with pain and itching and crawling for drugs.

Jodi slowly roused days later to the sound of machines beeping all around her. She looked around and realized that she was in hospital scrubs and tucked in tightly to a hospital bed with laundry-scented sheets. She tried to move her head but realized that she had a neck brace on. She had tubes in both arms, her nose, and between her legs. She felt a warm

hand on her forehead and saw a nurse beside her.

"Go to sleep," the nurse said.

Jodi was confused by the gentleness of the nurse's voice. She had always hated hospitals and had avoided them at all costs. She had had one terrible experience after another there. There was a guy named Jimmy who lived in a box off an alleyway on the strip. She had watched as he was repeatedly arrested for disturbing the peace. He was a lunatic, as he would walk up and down the streets, pushing a shopping cart down the road, hollering for Jesus. But they did not see Jimmy like she did. Jimmy was sweet and harmless. He would find nice items from his searches through the leftovers the rich had left behind and bring them to the girls. Nice coats, shoes, a bracelet, or a hair pin. He gave the girls any extra that he had.

The police would drop him off at the hospital, where staff would stabilize his schizophrenia with medication before kicking him back out onto the street. Jimmy had no money and no means to buy his medicine, and so after its effects had worn off, he became "the raving lunatic" again. Nothing but a crazy, homeless drunk. To the medical system, he was nothing but an inconvenience.

This had infuriated her, and she couldn't understand how people could not see the blatant double standard. She had sat in a waiting room and watched as a well-to-do white man in a dapper suit arrived on the arm of his doting wife, after suffering a panic attack at work. He was immediately seen by doctors after a few short minutes and given an x-ray,

ECG, and a whole battery of tests to ensure that he was okay. Meanwhile, she had sat in the waiting room for twelve hours while every other patient was seen before her, because she was "obviously" only there looking for drugs anyway. The hospital staff had eventually called the police on her because she was screaming in pain. They "knew" she was faking her pain, and as such, she was being a disturbance to the other patients. The police had escorted her from the premises with an appendix ready to burst.

She would never be the priority over the white woman who had a sore throat. They could care less if Jodi dropped dead from a heart attack on the waiting-room floor. The few times she had been seen by a doctor over the years, even the most seasoned among them put on two pairs of gloves and avoided touching her unless necessary. Ashamed, she had watched from a hospital bed as nurses turned up their noses at her and rolled their eyes at each other, complaining loudly about how bad she smelled.

"It's okay, sweetie," the nurse said again. "You can sleep. You are alright."

Having a nurse tell her go to sleep with any sort of civility, let along gentleness, could not possibly be right. She must have been beaten so badly, that they did not recognize the telltale signs of a drug addict. All thoughts quieted as she felt golden warmth trickle from her arm and down through her whole body. She closed her eyes and let sleep take her again.

As she floated on the periphery of sleep, Jodi heard a conversation nearby: two men, talking to a woman, in authoritative

voices. She did not dare open her eyes.

"Does she have any identification on her? Do you know her name?"

"No," said the nurse. "She has not even been awake for more than an hour in the past few weeks. Her nose and orbital bones were broken, and she has been severely concussed. She has a small bleed on her brain. It took thirty stitches to reconstruct her perineal area due to the extent of the damage. It will be a long time before she is ready to talk, but I will call you when she is in a more stable and alert state."

"Here is our card. This assault needs to be investigated before this sadist ups the ante and moves into our communities. No one has reported this one missing, so we are thinking by the look of her she is likely a prostitute. They never learn their lesson," he said rolling his eyes. "The results of the rape kit were positive for semen but did not match to anyone in our system. Speaking with her is the only way we will get any information about her attacker." From experience these sorts of people do not talk so probably a crap shoot."

"Yes, officer, I understand the importance. I promise that, as soon as she is able, I will call you directly."

Day and night blended. Jodi would wake up screaming, her body writhing in pain. The nurse would respond quickly, injecting more pain medication into her IV line. She would float away again until either the pain or withdrawals woke her back up. Rinse and repeat. Day in, day out.

She was being weaned off the pain medication now, and it was causing her physical agony. They had removed the IV

lines and were now giving her Percocet to manage the pain, combined with Tylenol 3's. Sometimes they would also give her an injection of Toradol when things were bad. In her desperation, she started to save her pain meds in her cheek and then store them in her pillowcase after the nurse left. When she had several saved up, she would crush and snort them.

Jodi's catheter had been removed, as she had proven herself able to get up to use the washroom unassisted, and she was even allowed to remove her neck brace for short periods at a time. It was decided that she was finally well enough to have a real bath instead of a sponge bath.

As the nurse prepared her bath, she carefully snorted her medicine, finishing just in time before the woman returned. The nurse escorted her to the bathroom and helped her into the hot water. Once she settled in the tub, the nurse left her to it, with a corded button to push when she was ready to get out, or if she needed help. Jodi nodded along with the instructions, doing her best to mask the effects of the drugs kicking in.

When she was finally alone, she let her heavy eyelids fall closed at last, sinking up to her shoulders into the blissful heat of the water, even as her mind started to drift ... further and further back in time...

1972

Jodi heard the clip of his smart shoes on the ceramic tiles. She watched as the shadow of a man appeared at the opening to their room. There was only one man in the facility, so she knew it must be Father Michael. He entered the room, and Jodi opened her eyelids a crack to watch him as he walked up and down the rows of sleeping girls, snug in their beds. Jodi heard him come closer and pass on her right side. She closed her eyes tight and breathed deeply to pretend she was asleep. She felt the swish of his cassock sweep against her arm, and her nose picked up the scent of his peppery aftershave. After a few moments had passed, she braved a little peek. Jodi could see him bent over Sarah's bed now, gently shaking her shoulder to rouse her. Sarah looked confused and disoriented upon awakening, but then bolted straight up in bed when she saw Father Michael.

"Father, is everything alright?" Sarah asked, alarmed.

Sarah scanned the room, looking for fire, smoke, or a sick and injured child. Jodi watched as her body slowly relaxed; all the little girls were safely tucked in.

"Come with me, Sarah," he whispered.

"Yes, Father. Of course," Sarah said while slipping her feet into her slippers and throwing on her robe. Jodi saw Father Michael put out his hand to her, and she watched Sarah hesitate slightly before reaching for it. His large hand swallowed her smaller one, and together they walked out of the room and down the hall.

Jodi was worried and afraid for Sarah. She must have done something bad, as only bad girls were sent to see Father Michael, after first being strapped mercilessly by the nuns. She and Sarah were best friends, and they told each other everything. She racked her brains, trying to remember the entire past week to see if there was something she had missed, but produced nothing. Sarah had been happy that week, and Jodi had not seen her get in trouble once with the nuns. It was odd that Father Michael would come to their room at this early hour to see her.

Perhaps the kitchen was short staffed and needed help preparing for breakfast in a few hours. That makes sense, she thought, but something still did not feel right. Jodi could not put a finger on what was wrong, but the feeling of unease remained nonetheless, steadily increasing the longer Sarah was gone. Her mind ran wildly astray with scenarios of where Sarah might be. Jodi was unable to fall asleep as her anxiety kicked into high gear and she lay there, tossing and turning for what felt like hours.

Jodi breathed in deeply and focused her attention on the rhythmic sound of the little girls gently snoring in their beds. She and Sarah were the oldest, and they did their best to comfort and care for the little ones. They still wept at night, asking for their mothers. She and Sarah would take turns singing to them and telling them stories. Each night, they would crawl into bed with them one by one to hold them, stroke their hair, and kiss their cheeks. It was all the love these girls would ever receive.

Jodi heard the scuff of Sarah's slippers returning to the room and looked up. Sarah's usually quick and nimble gait was slow and sluggish, as though she were limping. Her face was blanched and

twisted in a grimace of pain. She slowly and painfully crawled into her bed.

"Sarah, where did you go?" Jodi asked quietly. "Are you alright?"

Sarah responded by rolling away from her onto her side and curling herself up into a little ball. Jodi watched as Sarah's body started to tremble and shake. She heard Sarah whimper and choke up, burying her face in the pillow to muffle her cries. Jodi got quickly out of bed and crawled in beside her, holding her close and stroking her hair as Sarah cried and cried and cried. At some point, they both fell asleep.

They awoke to the sharp tapping of Sister Mary's shoes approaching the room, the sound angry and foreboding as always. All the girls immediately dropped to their knees and adopted the prayer position, facing the door. They said the Lord's Prayer in unison, each making the sign of the cross in perfect synchronicity. She and Sarah had practised this routine endlessly with the little ones to prevent them from receiving harsh discipline. If one of the little girls did make a mistake, she or Sarah would always do something extravagant to distract Sister, taking the punishment for the little one.

When the little ones would watch Sarah or Jodi being punished, tears running down their cheeks, both of the older girls would blink three times and twitch their noses twice, signaling to the girls to be strong, to be quiet, to bow their heads, to make no sounds or movement, and most important, to show no reaction to the beatings. They had taught them to grit their teeth, tighten their hands on the blankets and squeeze them hard, and sing or repeat a mantra loudly in their heads until it was over. Each time

this happened, the little girls would work harder and harder to perfect their morning routine to avoid the threat of punishment for anyone.

Sister Mary would walk sternly up and down the rows of beds, looking at each girl and slapping her thick, black-leather strap against the palm of her calloused hand as she passed. Any flinch would immediately be met with pain. She enjoyed doling it out, and there was almost no way to make it through the morning routine without someone being punished, no matter how perfect and still they tried to be. Despite their efforts, as time went on, the frequency of the beatings increased, as did the severity. Sister Mary had gotten a taste of power, and the more pain she inflicted, the more she grew to like it. It seemed as if she would almost leave her body during her fits of brutality. At times, she would become almost wild—primal—her eyes alight with malice. The punishments became increasingly unpredictable and had started to escalate beyond beatings to other horrific acts of torture. Sister Mary seemed to revel in her demented lust for complete power and control over the innocent and subservient children.

This morning, Sister Mary had made it through all the beds without one child being harmed. The feeling of tension was palpable in the air; small hearts beating out of little chests as the children prayed that Sister Mary was going to relent today. Their wish was almost granted. They watched as Sister Mary placed the strap back into the belt of her habit. There were only two beds left: Jodi's and Sarah's.

Sister Mary passed her bed and was almost past Sarah's when she stopped abruptly. Sister Mary looked up quickly and saw

that Sarah was starting to slump over where she knelt, her head was resting on the bed, and her arms hung down. She looked like she would topple over to the floor at any moment. Jodi saw Sister Mary draw the strap and knew she needed to take Sarah's beating.

Jodi had not been strapped in a while, and Sarah was surely in no shape to take one today. Jodi could almost feel the pain in Sarah's body. This morning, her face was pale, and her eyes completely absent of light. Sarah had not participated in the morning's conversations, nor had she answered any questions asked of her. Jodi had noticed that it had taken Sarah a long time to get down into the kneeling position, that she held her tummy as if in discomfort as she tried settle in, and that she even had dried brown stains on the back of her nightgown.

Jodi drew in a deep courageous breath, stood up beside her bed, and in a firm, loud voice, yelled, "Sister Mary, you smell like a dirty pig!"

She heard the little girls gasp behind her. Sister Mary froze, strap in hand for what seemed like forever. Then she turned on her heel and stared straight into Jodi's eyes, her throat and cheeks flushing bright red. Jodi saw the violence rising in Sister Mary's eyes, which glinted with revulsion and hate. Her face broke into a frighteningly sadistic smile that she carried with her as she stormed towards Jodi and forcefully shoved her, knocking her to the floor. The little girls started to whimper but silenced when Sister Mary turned sharply and stared them down. Sister Mary reached down and grabbed Jodi by the hair, yanking her firmly up to her feet, and dragging her to the shower at the front

of the room.

She ripped Jodi's clothes off then, screaming in pure rage, "You were born dirty! You are all nothing! You should have all been wiped from this bloody Earth!"

Jodi looked down at the little girls, blinking and twitching her nose, and smiled at them.

Sister Mary ordered four of the girls to the shower. They were scared but knew better than to disobey. Sister Mary ripped open the shower curtain and threw Jodi down on the floor. Stripped naked, she laid down on the cold tiles, chills running through her. Sister Mary ordered each girl to sit down on one of Jodi's arms and legs, holding it tight. Jodi felt the pressure and pain of their little bodies on her extremities.

Sister Mary turned on the ice-cold water then, immediately freezing her chest and stomach. Jodi could feel the little girls tense as they arched their backs to get away from the cold. Sister Mary then twisted the handle sharply and sent scalding hot water down on her. Jodi's screams filled the room. As Jodi screamed and cried, the little girls sitting on her tried to stand and let her up, but each was strapped hard as Sister Mary struck at them in a blind rage, connecting with whatever body part the strap found. The other little girls in the main room were now sobbing uncontrollably, wide-eyed and paralyzed with fear. Once or twice, one of them would try to move but cowered back to their beds as soon as their eyes met Sister Mary's.

Finally, Sister Mary turned the water off, looking down at Jodi as she lay in shock on the floor, simultaneously frozen and burned; then she raised her strap high above her head and rained

down blow after blow, whipping Jodi relentlessly and continuing long after she had lost consciousness.

CHAPTER 7

"Jodi? ... Wake up, sweetheart."

Jodi struggled to rouse. The nightmare had a hold of her and refused to let go. It grabbed at her threatening to pull her back in. Trembling and shivering, she finally managed to escape and return to reality. She looked up from the bath to find a deeply concerned nurse looking down at her.

"It is freezing in here. Let us get you back to bed."

The bath water had long since gone cold, and she gladly let the nurse help her out and dry her off.

Minutes later, Jodi was settled down onto her bed, comfortable but heartbroken, trying desperately to remember Sarah's face. As the nurse tucked her in, the murky image of a girl with a gap-toothed smile and freckles passed behind her closed eyes.

Over the next few weeks, Jodi began to heal and feel much more comfortable. The neck brace was gone for good. She was told that the minor brain injury had largely resolved itself, though they were still keeping a close eye on it, and the bones in her face were almost healed. There were still

yellowish purple bruises and angry-looking abrasions, but the swelling had gone down, and she almost looked like her old self. This morning would be her last scheduled dose of pain meds though, and her body was already starving for a fix. She could literally hear the flicking sound of a lighter, the bubbling of beautiful amber liquid, and feel the tautness of the rubber band around her arm. She had suffered long enough, and it was time to get back to work so she could get one step closer to nirvana.

She had started to familiarize herself with the nurses and their schedules. She had them categorized: nurse one—detailed, strict, firm, and organized; nurse two—pushover, nice to a fault, easily convinced to give her more pain meds; nurse three—cold, did her job but with absolutely no bedside manner; and nurse four—sloppy, overweight, super gentle and nice, but didn't pay a lot of attention as she was always in a rush and running around like a chicken without its head.

The sloppy nurse, Michelle, was on the morning shift that day. When she arrived, she told Jodi that she had talked to the police to let them know that her health had improved enough that she was ready to assist in the investigation. She had told Jodi that they would be there at noon. In that moment, Jodi knew it was now or never, and she began to rehearse scenario after scenario in her head, running through the pros and cons of each.

Anxiety crept in and began intensifying to outright panic. Every plan she came up with had serious flaws, and the chance of her escaping was next to nil. If she failed, she would be

formed and observed twenty-four hours a day, and without pain meds to at least crush and snort, she would rather die. She finally chose the best scenario and prepared to take the risk.

She never ended up having to use it though because the Universe handed her a golden opportunity she had never imagined, let alone planned for. Just before shift change, Michelle rolled in with the medication cart. Jodi watched anxiously as Michelle put the keys into the cabinet that stored the narcotics and opened it up. Just as Michelle began to pull out the drawer though, an alarm blared over the PA system, startling them both.

"CODE BLUE! ROOM 307!
CODE BLUE! ROOM 307!"

Without another thought, Michelle—the only nurse on the wing for the next few minutes—took off running out the door to attend to the life-threatening situation. Without hesitation, Jodi hopped out of bed and ran to the medication cart, ripping open the narcotic drawer and stuffing her pockets with as many vials and bottles as she could. Just before she turned to leave, she saw Michelle's stethoscope and grabbed it as well, slinging it around her neck.

The halls were clear, though Jodi could hear the commotion of incoming staff responding to the Code Blue from the far end. She walked nonchalantly to the elevator, feeling a slight twinge of guilt for Michelle, knowing she'd be in big trouble when they found out that Jodi and all the narcotics were gone.

The elevator arrived, and she brushed off the feeling, stepping inside and pressing the ground-floor button. Dressed in hospital scrubs and carrying a stethoscope, she was just another nurse, doctor, or intern walking by. No one so much as looked at her as they bustled off to their appointments.

Up ahead was a small in-hospital café that offered warm treats, tables where people could rest and discuss the situation they were in with their loved ones, or just grab a quick snack or meal. Jodi noticed a table of four elderly woman chatting over coffee, fully absorbed in one of the women's stories. They were gripping their hearts and offering sympathetic and consoling words.

As Jodi approached, she noticed that one of the women who had her back to her had slung her large leather purse over the side of her chair. Jodi scanned her surroundings and picked up a half empty bottle of water someone had discarded on one of the tables behind the women. With one last look around her for threats, Jodi threw the water bottle as hard as she could against the wall opposite the women. Startled, everyone in the coffee shop looked to the wall, and Jodi seized the opportunity to grab the purse from the woman's chair and slowly walk outside the hospital through the turnstile.

Laughing to herself at how easy it had all been, and barely believing her luck, Jodi jumped into the first cab she saw—in a line of them parked outside the hospital. She directed the driver to take her to a store near one of the cheap motels she often stayed at, which was also close to one of her drug

connections.

While they drove, she opened the purse and started rifling through it. She opened the wallet inside and gasped when she found a huge stack of bills. She estimated there was close to five hundred dollars in there. Any guilt she was feeling about Michelle was long gone now as she imagined what she could do with the money.

In did not take long before they pulled up outside the store. Jodi paid the driver in cash and quickly got out. When he pulled away, she went through her pockets, threw all the vials and pill bottles into the purse, and then walked hurriedly to the store, popping a handful of Percocet just before swinging open the convenience store door. Jodi knew that she would be getting real dope soon, and the anticipation and excitement fluttered in her chest. She had only taken the pills to buy her time to get some food. She had no intention of leaving the motel room again anytime soon once she got her fix.

As Jodi headed towards the motel, carrying the staples: smokes, potato chips, and two sixty-ounce bottles of vodka, she saw Dino standing outside it with his back up against the wall. Before leaving the convenience store, she had pulled just enough money to pay for her dope. She had even made sure to crumple up her dope money to make it look as though she had scrounged for every dollar needed to pay for her fix. Nothing good ever happened if it was known that you were

flushed with cash on street.

Dino nodded to her and turned to walk behind the motel. She walked in the opposite direction, and they met each other behind an old, rusted sea container parked out back.

"Jesus, Jodi, you look like hell! Where were you? And what are you wearing? Everyone has you written off as dead!

Jodi looked down and realized she was still wearing hospital scrubs.

"Dino, it's a long story," she said, trying to crack a reassuring smile.

"Well, I bet it is. You will have to tell me some time," he said, his curiosity piqued. "How you paying, doll? Cash or tricks?"

"Cash this time, Dino. You know you like to wait for it." Jodi smiled, pushing his shoulder playfully.

Dino laughed and shook his head, and they made the exchange. "Until next time, doll face," he said mockingly as she turned towards the motel.

"Hey, Jodi," Dino called after her in a serious voice. "Are you going to be okay?"

She looked back at him, recognizing genuine concern in his eyes.

"Now, Dino, don't you be getting all emotional. You know the hustle. It is what it is, baby." With that, she started walking away.

"Okay, girl, but I'll be checking up on you. Room 202?"

"You know me," she said, still walking, "always predictable, but if you want a piece, you are paying for it ... and you better bring a pizza. I will leave the porch light on," she added

playfully, "and the key under the mat."

"You truly are something else, girl," Dino called, watching her open the door to the hotel lobby. "Bye!"

Jodi smiled softly, touched by his obvious concern for her, though not truly surprised. Although it would seem foreign to those who had never walked down the path of true misfortune, even on the outer fringes of society, people were interconnected, not only by greed or addiction but by a common thread of understanding and survival. There was care, concern, compassion, and love to be found even between those rotten apples that have fallen—or been shaken—from society's tree.

At the end of the day, she thought, *who else do we have to rely on?*

They were all just trying their best to survive. It was just unfortunate for the afflicted and addicted that the very thing that kills them was also the thing that kept them alive.

The pills were kicking in now, so Jodi jumped eagerly off that negative train of thought and just rode the wave. As she walked up to the main entrance, she shook a crisp white smoke out of the pack—a pleasant change from the usual crushed and dirty butts she would fish from some outdoor ashtray. She placed it between her lips, lit it, and took in a satisfying drag. She was okay. She had money, food, shelter, and her drugs. She could barely wait to get to her room.

"Let me guess. Room 202?" said the older man behind the desk, laughing pleasantly.

"Oh, you know me too well, Larry." She smiled at him and

handed over enough cash for the week.

"And you are alone? Business slowing down before the cold?"

"Always does," she answered with a shrug. "Which is a wonder, really. You would think they'd want help staying warm." She chuckled at her own joke, finding everything quite amusing suddenly.

He smiled. "Haven't seen you in a while, kiddo, and your pretty face.... Well, you look like you've been through the ringer," he said, his brows furrowed with worry.

"A girl has to keep her secrets, but I'm still standing." She straightened a bit, trying to look like she was as okay as she claimed. "Going to take a few days to rest before I got to hit the streets again though."

"You need anything, kiddo, you just ask. You know we are always here for you. Sheila will even whip you up a nice meal." He looked like a grandfather, looking at her with clear affection, his glasses on the tip of his nose.

"Thanks, Larry. I just need some sleep. Actually, is there any chance that Sheila has some extra jogging pants and a t-shirt? Maybe some extra toiletries?"

He looked at her clothing. It was stained in places with what looked like old blood, and she looked more than just disheveled. It was clear that she had been in the hospital after suffering what had likely been a brutal beating.

"Hold on, darling. I am sure we can find you something." Jodi took a seat in the lobby to wait, and he returned only a little while later with a laundry basket full of stuff for her:

clean pajamas, t-shirts, sweaters, pants, socks, shoes, and a toiletry bag full of soaps. On top of the basket was a large bottle of water, homemade cookies, and a plate of fruit. Stunned, she looked at him with tears running down her face. "Larry.... This is too much."

He gave her a pat on the shoulder, "You need it, and you deserve it. Go get cleaned up and get some sleep, kiddo." He placed the key to her room on top of her laundry basket and watched as she walked down the hall, glancing back at him several times. He smiled at her and shooed her off to her room, throwing up a silent prayer for her. Even after she was out of sight, he could not stop worrying, fiddling with his key chain, and feeling something that he couldn't quite nail down. Was it helplessness? Hopelessness? Guilt? Sorrow? Whatever he was feeling, it definitely wasn't comfortable. He sighed with resignation. As much as he wanted to help, he knew it wasn't his business to interfere in her life and trying to would only serve to push her away.

Larry was proud of his motel, and it served as a safe haven for those in need, but still.... It was difficult not to become emotionally attached to the people who walked through its doors. Seldom was their outcome positive, and with every loss he suffered, his heart broke a little more.

A former combat medic, long retired, he was well-off and certainly had not opened this place for the money. He had just wanted to help. Years ago, he had met Sheila, a nurse, in a downtown shelter. At the time, booze and drugs were the only thing that kept the demons he'd brought back from

the war at bay. She had seen the good in him that he could not see himself anymore, and it had saved his life. *She* had saved his life.

Once he'd gotten a grip on his addiction, and started working his recovery on a daily basis, the universe had opened up to him in serendipitous ways. One unbelievable opportunity after another had presented itself to him and Sheila, eventually providing them with a profitable life thanks to a variety of property and business ventures. Despite their financial success though, their hearts were still with the addicts, with people who were unable to get up and stay on their feet due to circumstances they had never asked to be in.

Their dream had always been to open a safe house, or sober-living home, to give back to those in need, offering them a safe, warm roof over their heads, and support if requested. As they were keeping an eye out for potential properties, Sheila had stumbled upon this motel. Together, they'd tried to legally wade through all the Government red tape to licence it for use as a safe house of some sort, but of course, the bureaucrats had made the process impossibly difficult. He and Sheila had finally discussed their options, and decided that it was best to leave the place as a cheap, pay-by-the hour motel, which would attract those living in high-risk lifestyles in any case, and give them the chance to provide kindness and support to anyone who needed it, especially those in the throes of addiction.

Larry and Sheila did not label the motel in any way or advertise it as being affiliated to addiction or mental-health services. That would only serve to scare away those most in need.

Everyone who came to the motel for whatever reason—be it drugs, tricks, sleep, shower, or escape—was welcome. Their clients had no idea that they were being actively supported or fed specifically to assist them in survival. They just saw it as a cheap motel where they could stay without judgement.

Larry and Sheila always had coffee, snacks, and hot soups ready and available. They made sure that every room had clean needles, as well as fully stocked first-aid kits, including Narcan and contraceptives. All the rooms were the same, and on the back of every door hung a large paperwork folder, filled with pamphlets, contact numbers, and resources for things like social assistance, safe housing, abortions, blood testing, medical care, and clinics specializing in a variety of services in the community that could help if required.

And most importantly, in the reception area, there was a dry-erase board announcing events held in the activity room, such as AA, NA, and CA meetings. Most of the time, those meetings were empty, aside from Larry himself, but he was always there to listen ready to listen to whomever needed to talk.

He and Sheila tried their best to do all they could do to help. Even if it took twenty years to help one person turn their life around, they knew it would be worth it. Larry took Jodi's cash and put it in an envelope. He would have the housekeeper hide it in her purse, jacket, or bag. He had just always had a special space in his heart for Jodi.

Jodi simply could not comprehend the compassion and generosity of Larry and Sheila. As she walked down the hall

towards her room, she felt guilty, knowing she was going to her room to get high and that there was no way she could stop that from happening.

As she looked back at Larry, for a moment, she thought to herself, *what if I don't? What if I run back to him, spill it all out, and ask them to help me?*

It saddened her that she knew the answer. The devil had its claws dug into her too deeply. She had no self-control left in her and hadn't for a very long time. Her desire to get high overrode any thought of getting clean. She couldn't have stopped herself even if she'd truly wanted to.

Jodi could barely get the key in the door, dropping it on the floor more than once; her hands were shaking badly with excitement and her body on fire with want. Once Jodi got inside the room, she quickly popped another handful of pills to buy some time. Even though every fibre of her being screamed for dope, she still wanted to romanticize the experience. She wanted to make sure everything was set up perfectly so that she could savour every moment.

She grabbed the bottle of vodka and downed gulp after gulp. The booze immediately filled her body with golden warmth. Jodi ran to take a shower then, checking that task off the list. She knew that this was likely her last shower for several days, and she wanted to wash herself thoroughly. The booze and pills started to mix and go to her head then, relaxation coursing through her body, her hunger for the dope temporarily abated.

She took another big swig of vodka, then climbed into

the shower's stream of hot, soothing water. Looking down, she saw that her legs were still covered in yellowish purple bruising. Taking a deep breath, she traced her finger over the jagged pattern of stitching between her legs, feeling more stitches than she could count, each of them required to repair the jagged tears and pull her tissues back together. She was nowhere near the point where she was ready to work, but she knew she could only afford a few more days off, even with the cash she had stolen.

Jodi would have to find a way to switch things up; pulling quick tricks until her body had healed properly, or at least enough. The money wasn't near as good, but she could get through each John faster, squeezing more work into less time. She knew that she couldn't risk an infection because there was absolutely no way she could go back to the hospital again.

Jodi finished her shower as quick as she could and jumped out and changed into the clean pajamas before picking up the motel phone and dialing Dino's number. There was no answer, and her call went straight to voicemail.

"Dino, its Jodi. Could you pop over two or three days from now? I'll need a replenishment by then. And don't forget the pizza either. The doors open." She realized that she was slurring a bit, the cocktail in her bloodstream beginning to kick into high gear.

She put the "Do Not Disturb" sign on the outer doorknob so she would not be interrupted, stuffed her face with Sheila's cookies and started to prepare her fix. The anticipation was eating her alive, her hands shaking worse than ever with

restless excitement, making it almost impossible to go slow and be careful. Finally, the moment arrived.

Jodi tied the rubber around her arm and primed the syringe, watching the small bead of bliss glistening in the light at the end of the needle. Her tolerance would have decreased significantly over the past weeks in the hospital; she knew that. She was also fully snowed already from the booze, mixed with the stolen pain pills.

She knew she would have to start small and increase gradually, but she had difficulty restraining herself from injecting her usual dose. She knew it wouldn't take long for her tolerance to build back up, and then she'd have to hustle her ass off to replenish her supply. She took a deep breath, her heart racing, and pierced her vein, collapsing almost immediately back against the pillows. The pain in her body and heart disappeared as intense waves of pleasure swept over her.

The warmth of the dope had long since worn off. Her sweat had soaked the sheets, and she had awoken frozen and shivering, with chills rippling through her. She reached quickly over to the bedside table and took a healthy swallow of pills, washing them down with more vodka, then stumbled to the bathroom in an uncoordinated daze

Once she had finished and was back in clean dry clothes, she stripped the soaking wet bed sheets, and then crawled back into bed, swallowing another huge mouthful of Vodka before getting things ready and shooting up again.

Jodi floated, nodding in and out of a dream-like state in an endless loop as repetitive as it was inevitable: sleep, dope, maybe eat, then repeat. Between the heroin, the alcohol, and the painkillers, she slipped helplessly into a trance with no concept of time or place. The smell of vomit and piss, mingling together, permeated the air but did not reach her anymore.

It had been almost two days, and Dino had not heard a peep from Jodi. He knew she had cash too, and he needed it. He had a surplus of supply he needed to move before he was late for his deadline. He was on the lowest bar of the drug ring, and shit runs downhill. He grabbed a pizza, booze, and smokes and headed off to see her.

Dino walked into the motel—the little bell jingling over-head, announcing his presence—and headed down to Jodi's room. He knocked, calling her name. No answer. He pounded harder on the door. The door had been locked, even though she said she would leave it open. She must have gone out to pull a few tricks. He would wait around for a bit to see if she returned. He walked down to the front desk.

"Pizza, pizza, come and get your pizza!" He bellowed.

Larry came out from the back. "Dino, my boy! I would never turn down pizza! How you doing? You need a room for the night?" he asked happily. Larry loved Dino. He was funny and caring, a good boy beneath it all. He was a breath

of fresh air really, and his personality filled the room. He would sit with him and Sheila for hours sometimes, playing cards and making them laugh.

"Nah, I don't need a room," he said. "I'm actually here to look for Jodi. I was supposed to check in on her but haven't heard nothing from her in a few days. Doors locked to her room, and no answer. She must be out working tonight?"

Larry picked up the phone and dialed her room. No answer. "You know what, we have not seen her either. Not unusual, of course, but she was in rough shape when she checked in."

"Yeah, someone gave her a good one," Dino said. "Do you mind if we check it out? If she is gone, nothing to worry about."

Larry put the key in the door but knocked again several times before entering. She might just be in the shower or turning tricks, and he wouldn't want to pop in on her in the middle of either. Still nothing. He put his ear to the door. All was quiet. Hopefully, she was just out, having left late at night or in the early morning. But just in case....

The door was not even open a crack before the smell of vomit punched him in the face. He was not able to fully open the door because there was a body lying face up behind it, blocking his access.

"Jesus! Jodi?!" Dino yelled.

They pushed their way in, and the scene that greeted them was beyond unpleasant. Jodi had dry vomit caked on her cheek and chin. Her skin was chalky white, and her lips were tinged blue. They had both seen this a time or two, and the

outcome was generally grim. Larry felt her wrist and detected a faint pulse.

"Grab the Narcan!" Larry yelled.

Dino ripped open the cupboard, fumbling through the supplies, tossing them all to the floor in frustration and panic. He finally grabbed the Narcan pouch off the floor and ran back to Larry, tripping over the bed in his haste.

"Rip it open and spray inside each nostril," Larry ordered, his voice surprisingly calm given the situation. This wasn't his first rodeo. Larry started chest compressions, followed by rescue breaths.

Jodi came around immediately, gasping, her eyes wild. He knew she wasn't out of the woods yet though. Not by a long shot. Not only would withdrawal kick in immediately, but in fifteen minutes, the Narcan would wear off, and she could go right back into overdose. She became aggressive and combative towards them then, realizing what they had done: They had killed her high. Dino straddled her, sitting on her thighs and holding her arms and legs tightly. Larry went to the door and yelled out to Sheila, who came running. She rounded the hallway just a few seconds later, and entered the room, taking in the situation before locking eyes with her husband.

No words passed between them as she turned immediately, running back into the hall. As Jodi screamed and did her best to fight them, several more people opened their doors and looked towards Jodi's room. The clientele that frequented the establishment knew exactly what was happening and

moved in quickly to help. Sheila came running back then with sheets. They wrapped the sheets tightly around her, and they all gathered to help lift her up and restrain her from kicking and fighting. Finally, she had been contained within tight wrappings and the hands of several people holding onto her.

"Room 205!" Sheila yelled, and together, they carried her to the other room and held her down while they placed the towels around her wrists and ankles and secured her tightly to the bed. Jodi arched her back, screaming and screaming as she fought helplessly against her restraints. The fighting went on for what felt like hours. She was soaked in sweat and writhing like a woman possessed, spitting at them, and wildly screaming every swear word that ever there was. She rained down upon them a venomous fury of hate.

After some time passed, she finally began to quiet, still not ready to stop the fight but too exhausted to keep it up much longer. Eventually, her screams turned to whimpers, and not long after that, she fell into a deep sleep. Everyone felt relieved.

"Thank you, everyone," Larry said to them, profoundly grateful. "Thank you all so much." This band of seeming misfits had bonded together to save one of their own, and no matter what road you walk in this life, which was admirable. They all offered their support, and to return if needed, before retiring to their own rooms. Larry watched them all go, resigned to the fact that many of them would still get high on their drug of choice once they were back in their rooms, the evening's happenings already fading from their minds.

Larry, Dino, and Sheila took turns watching Jodi. Most people who OD'd were okay without treatment after close monitoring for an hour, but they decided to sit with her through the night. No one called the police. She was going to be okay and calling the cops would just bring about fear in an already terrorized community. The motel was a safe, welcoming place where people could live their life without judgment. He and Sheila were able to manage the most common drug-related injuries due to their combined medical backgrounds. Their storage room in back was full of medical supplies and emergency equipment.

Sheila had a friend at the hospital who had given her expired over-the-counter medicines, sedatives, and antibiotics. They were prepared for about everything. There were occasions when emergencies necessitated a call to the police or ambulance, but in these cases, the person was beyond saving. Larry tried to only invoke this as a last option. Police and hospitals ask questions, and both Larry and Sheila could be implicated if it were discovered that they were allowing illegal activity on their premises, let alone performing medical interventions without a licence. If he could remove the person from the premises without violence or drive them to the hospital calling an ambulance on the way, he would.

Throughout the night, Jodi slept off and on, cycling between fits of crying and begging. She was sweating, and her face was green. They gave her small sips of water and held popsicles to her lips. Eventually she was more compliant, especially with the promise of a fix. Larry paid Dino for the dope and his

time, as well as the money he needed to keep his superiors at bay, He and Dino would spend the next twenty-four hours with Jodi, managing her dose and keeping her comfortable.

Jodi watched as they injected the dope, immediately quelling her nausea and relaxing her. Coolness misted over her, and she felt coherent but relaxed.

"Jodi, I'm going to untie your restraints now," Sheila said gently from her seat beside the bed, "and help you use the washroom. Then we're going to get you washed up and fed. If you remain calm and non-violent, you'll continue to be given your fix."

Jodi saw the kindness and warmth in her eyes, a never-ending fountain of compassion, and nodded. She rubbed her wrists and ankles as the restraints came off. Sheila held her tightly and assisted her from the bed into the bathroom. She turned on the water for a bath and added bubbles. While it was filling up, she stripped off Jodi's clothes.

"Get in, doll," she said lovingly as she sat on the corner of the tub. "Soak it all away,"

The former nurse then helped her wash her body and hair, noticing her wince as she washed her intimate areas.

"Does that hurt?"

Jodi nodded, her eyes full of tears.

"Do you mind if I take a look?"

Jodi thought about it and then shrugged her assent. It wasn't the first time someone had looked at her, and it wouldn't be the last. Besides, she trusted Sheila and knew she wouldn't hurt her. Sheila toweled her off and led her to

the bed. "Lie down, honey," Sheila said, fluffing her pillows and placing them under her head. "Just settle in, give in to the dope, and relax. I will not hurt you."

Jodi took a deep breath and tried to remain calm, even though the dope had started to wear off, so she couldn't lean into it as much as she felt she needed to. Sheila placed a sheet over her, tucking it tight under her armpits to afford her some level of privacy. Finally, she lifted the bottom of the covering, pulling it back towards Jodi's waist. She gasped then. "Oh, Jodi, my love.... I am so sorry." Sheila had never seen something so terrible and shuddered to think about what Jodi must have gone through.

A few minutes later, after knocking quietly, Larry walked in. "How you doin', beautiful?"

He didn't get an answer, but he didn't need one. The look on Jodi's face and the sadness in her eyes made it plain. He knelt at her bedside and pulled out a rubber tourniquet and syringe. Jodi looked at him gratefully. "Just a little, kiddo. Just enough to tie you over."

She nodded. Something was better than nothing. He kissed her on the forehead and left.

Sheila came back in then, carrying a stool, a headlamp, and medical instruments. "Jodi, your stitches are ready to come out."

Jodi closed her eyes, riding the high, and nodded that she was ready too. Sheila got right down to business. What seemed like hours later, she finally pulled the last stitch, then disinfected the area and applied an antibiotic salve

before bringing her a fresh clean pair of pajamas and helping her into them.

Jodi already felt much better, and thanked Sheila endlessly for her care.

"There is no need for thanks, sweetheart. Just get better. Sit up now. I will detangle your hair and braid it for you before you fall asleep."

Sheila moved behind her, running a brush gently through her hair. Jodi felt her shoulders relax as the dope and the gentle touch of another calmed her, and she drifted into a peaceful cloud.

1972

They took her. The men. They didn't even give her time to adjust before they had ripped the clothes from her body. She screamed as they threw the beautiful clothing her mother had made her into the fireplace. She watched, sobbing uncontrollably, as the flames consumed them, until she was slapped hard across the face by Sister Mary.

Jodi was thrown in a hot bath then and vigorously scrubbed until her skin burned. Next, Sister Mary roughly picked through her hair, scratching her scalp and ripping chunks of hair from her head.

"You have to check these little bastards," Sister Mary said to Sister Margret. "They're full of lice. This one is clear, surprisingly, but I'm going to treat it anyway. Better safe than sorry. I do not want whatever it has."

Jodi could see the shocked dismay on Sister Margaret's face as harsh cream was poured on Jodi's head. It dripped down her ears, neck, and face, burning little rivers of skin off as it went. Her head was pushed forcefully under the water, then she was pulled back to the surface by her hair, choking on the water, only to have Sister Mary shove her back under again.

"Surely, this isn't required!" exclaimed Sister Margaret, her eyes wide with alarm. "Please, let her go! She has had enough!"

"I will stop when I have had enough," Sister Mary barked. Understand this Sister Margaret, it is not worth the money it

costs to feed it. If one chokes to death, it will be one less problem to contend with.

Sister Mary yanked Jodi out of the tub and threw her an itchy wool blanket. Jodi wrapped herself in it, frozen and wet, and was slammed down hard onto a chair. Then Sister Mary came up behind her with a large pair scissors and tugged on her braid, pulling her head back.

"No, no please! Please don't cut it!" Jodi wailed. She looked pleadingly to Sister Margaret, who stood frozen. Without a single moment of hesitation, Sister Mary crudely hacked off her beautiful hair. Jodi wailed as she watched the thick, beautiful braid fall to the floor. Once again, she was slapped.

"You get control of yourself right now!" Sister Mary screamed, with nothing but cold hatred in her eyes. "The next time you have an outburst, I will whip you!" She pulled a black leather strap out of her belt then and snapped it sharply, demonstrating the force with which it could be wielded.

Jodi withered in fear at the cracking sound, which bought a smile to Sister Mary's face. Jodi put her head down then and resigned herself to her fate. She was tossed a nightgown, soap, a toothbrush, and some toothpaste, and was ushered to the girl's dormitory. Shell shocked, she just stood there as the door was slammed behind her. Dozens of little girls solemnly stared at her. A beautiful girl, around her age, walked towards her, smiling.

"I'm Sarah," she said, wrapping her arms around Jodi in a gesture of comfort. "It's going to be okay. I pinky promise. Let's get you settled. How old are you?"

"Twelve," Jodi replied.

"Me too!" With that, Sarah pulled her towards the other little girls.

CHAPTER 8

1991

"Shhhhh..." Still behind Jodi, Sheila was holding her in her arms and rocking her as she sobbed. "Shhhhh.... I know, dear. You've been through hell...."

After Jodi had calmed a bit, Sheila gave he r painkillers and tucked her into bed. Larry came in a few hours later and gave her another fix. Once again, Jodi drifted off.

She awoke alone a few hours later. It was dark, and she desperately needed a fix. She slowly padded down the motel's long hallway. There was no one in sight. She stopped and stared long and hard at the cash register at the front desk. It would be so easy to just empty it out, but she could not quite make herself take Larry and Sheila's money to score when they had just done so much for her. It was an extremely near thing, however. She knew that a time would come when every ounce of restraint would leave her once again, and she would do whatever was needed to survive. For now, though, she was hanging onto that restraint by the skin of her teeth.

She had scared herself this time, knowing full well how close

she had come to death and that she had to take things slow. Ideally, she would stop, of course, but she'd learned the hard way how sick she'd get without the dope. Her skin would start to crawl, and she would itch and sweat. The nausea would overwhelm her until she fell on her knees and heaved all she had. Soaked in sweat and bedridden—if she were lucky enough to have a bed—she would wait for death to come knocking at her door—if she were lucky enough to have a door.

Perhaps, she'd be able to call someone who would come and give her just enough to pull her out of death's grip, keeping her above ground for another day. They would then leave her lying in her own filth to replace or replenish the stash they had generously shared with her. If she weren't so lucky, the call would go unanswered. No matter how close she was with other addicts, the dope would always be their first priority. They would willingly sign your death warrant by choosing to hoard their precious supply.

She couldn't even blame them. When she was flying high, the furthest thing from her mind was the survival of someone else. Her body and mind would slowly shut down and blanket her in a warm cloud—a cloud so comforting that she wouldn't even realize she was sleeping on the ground in sub-zero weather, or being robbed, raped, or beaten. In that cloud, she would gladly choke on her own puke and be grateful that her long miserable life was finally over.

Jodi was permanently stuck in the cycle. Avoiding the sickness was just as important, just as compelling, as chasing the high. After a while, the two blended until she did not know

where one started and the other began.

Tearing her gaze from the cash register, unsure how long she had been standing there, fixated upon it, she forced herself to turn away and head to the door. As she reached for it, she noted the narrow rack of pamphlets that stood off to one side—the same pamphlets that hung from the door in every room.

On one of her earlier visits, Jodi had read one of them as she was killing time before a scheduled meeting with Dino. It had described her addiction perfectly and even explained why it had such a hold on her, which up until that point, she had never understood. The pamphlet had explained that people's brains make something called dopamine, which is a natural way for the body to feel nice and happy. If she were to win a race, for example, or pet a kitten, dopamine would give her this warm, happy feeling naturally. The dope imitated this feeling, but far quicker and exponentially stronger.

And it all came nicely packaged in a little syringe. One dose would take her to levels of euphoria that she would never get if she ran a thousand marathons. An addict like her would keep using just to feel that way over and over, even without the sickness of withdrawal acting as an extra unavoidable push.

And around and around it goes, she thought as she headed out into the cold, dark street. Jodi needed the dope to survive. This was the price she paid, and rent was due every day. She would do anything to get it, even if it meant she would sleep outside in the cold, starving.

She used to wish she could explain it to the people who would sneer at her and condescendingly suggest that she simply stop, but she knew they would never understand. Not the addiction itself and not why anyone would ever take that first hit, to confident were they that they would never end up in the same shoes.

Jodi had not woken up one day and decided to become an addict. No one ever makes that choice. Not the five-year-old, brought up in a trap house, witnessing indescribable horrors daily and ends up cutting drugs for his parents before he is even ten. before he is ten. Not the sixteen-year-old from a well-to-do family who breaks his leg skiing and is given Percocet; then refill after refill until he is crushing and snorting them before moving on to the "hard stuff."

If he is lucky, he dies of an OD in his bedroom, Jodi thought, leaving his parents with a bunch of questions with no answers. If he isn't lucky, he'll fail out of school, get kicked out of his house, and finally be exiled as everyone that ever loved him gives up on him, one after another. The rich kid ends up on the street with the rest of us, just trying to survive and waiting to die.

Every addict has a story. Jodi had hers, and she had learned countless others over the years. Every person—regardless of where they came from or what resources they might have at their disposal—was only a few bad choices, a few bad breaks, from ending up exactly like her. She just wished people could see that while they were still on the other side of it and be as eager to help as they were to turn up their noses and look the other way.

Jodi wandered up and down the freezing streets, frigid wind tore at her fingers, ears, and nose. Her feet, stuffed into knee-high leather boots that were a size too small, had long since gone numb. She knew she should return to the motel, but she needed money. Yes, she had a place to stay, and food, but the stolen cash from the old woman's purse would not last forever, and she would need more to replenish her dope supply. The sympathy card would only work for so long with Dino, becoming less effective the more she recovered.

At some point over the last several days, a heavy snow had fallen and been ploughed into dirty banks along the sidewalks. Jodi wore a light pea coat that stopped at mid-thigh and was not doing much in the way of keeping her fish-netted legs warm. In this occupation though, it did not pay to be overdressed no matter what the weather. The less clothes worn, the more clients you attracted. Braving the weather was what was needed to survive, and for the most part the ladies were acclimatized to these conditions. At some point though, it was just too unbearable for even the most seasoned. Most of the businesses on the strip were warm and welcoming, and would let you pop in here and there for warmth, but she never wanted to overstay her welcome and lose those privileges.

The freezing wind took Jodi's breath away. Her bones were ice. Even her soul felt cold. She checked her pockets. Half

a bottle of Percocet, and a few bumps of coke. In her other pocket, she had a few sampler bottles of whisky, and a half pack of smokes. It was not ideal, but it would get her through until the morning. There was no way she could brave the cold any longer.

She entered a grocery store up ahead, thinking that maybe if she warmed herself up for a half hour, she could work for just a little bit longer. She walked up and down the aisles, taking her time, slowly letting her blood thaw and start flowing again. She stopped in one of the aisles, looking at feminine hygiene products that she could not afford. She prayed, as she did every month, that she would be lucky, and her cycle would continue. While she compared the costs, she couldn't help but overhear a conversation between two women in the next aisle over, talking about a friend of theirs who'd started drinking too much after her husband left her.

"I know, right? The pitiful thing. But at least she was finally able to admit she needed help."

"Thank God. Too bad she had to wrap her car around a tree before she came to that conclusion though."

"True, but still ... I think it was so brave of Lindsey to admit that she had a problem and get some help."

In near disbelief, Jodi listened as they went on and on about what an inspiration Lindsey was and how proud they were of her.

What was the difference between her and Lindsey? Why was she a junkie whore and Lindsey some sort of icon to recovery? Shaking her head and retreating to a different

aisle, she wondered why no one even blinked when wealthy professionals drank too much or snorted line after line of coke. *Probably 'cause they can just pop into their Gucci recovery centres, be admired for doing so, and spend their days doing yoga and getting massages until the shakes go away. Like a reward to look forward to when they started using again.*

These were the same people—the same addicts—who walked by Jodi and people like her without so much as a glance of recognition, without concern. Her addiction was below theirs because she sat in tattered clothing, and wore a face stained with drug use, while they wore a three-piece suit and washed themselves with a hundred-dollar creams.

She was still shaking her head at the hypocrisy and injustice of it all when she left the grocery store and headed back out into the cold. As she rounded the corner, she heard the whoop of a police siren and saw the flash of red and blue lights.

Great, just what I need, she thought, defeated. She was no stranger to the cops or their laughable motto: "To serve and protect." That code did not apply to people like her, the seedy underbelly of society. They were the very people from whom the police worked so hard to protect their own from. If a beautiful, young white girl went missing on her university campus there would be amber alerts, posters, volunteers, and even a task force to bring her home safe. Of course, the woman deserved every effort that could possibly be made to find her, as every missing person should. But if Jodi or any of her sisters went missing? Well, that was just one less junkie whore.

If the cops bothered to investigate, the best they might do is dig up the latest drug-ravaged photo of the victim and broadcast it on the news to be disregarded by viewers by the next commercial break.

"Well, what did they think would happen to them?"

"Who cares? How is that our problem? They chose to put themselves in that situation."

They thought it would be better if those sorts of victims remained missing, or better yet, had taken a few friends with them. One less stain on society. Women like her, especially the Nation's most beautiful Indigenous sisters, had gone missing by the hundreds and yet both the police and society denied that there was an issue. Missing-person reports were frequently ignored, as was the advice of professional profilers attempting to uncover what could be happening to these women. And then, when victims were found chopped up and buried on some farm, the police were quick to make excuses and shift blame. To cover from their blunder, they "polished" their policies and named a memorial highway after them.

Problem solved. Crisis averted. More attention given to the murderer than their victims.

Jodi watched with dull resignation as the cop car pulled up close to her and stopped. She was clearly prostituting, and she knew that there was likely a warrant out for her arrest after that business at the hospital. One look at her priors, and she was done for. Jodi was in no condition to run, and at that point, she truly didn't care anymore. She had nothing left and knew that the world would not miss her in the slightest.

Why would it? She was nothing but the punching bag for misogyny—a creative outlet for the depravity of men, who would pick her up on the street where she waited for them, attractively packaged for their consumption and willing to meet any of their demands.

At least, in jail, she would have clean clothes and sleep in a warm, albeit uncomfortable bed. She'd have three meals a day, and ironically, easier access to drugs without having to suffer the perils of the streets to get them. There would be some beat downs, of course, but it wouldn't be worse than anything she'd already gone through. Eventually, she would be courted and tucked under the gentle arms of another woman, safe and loved. Maybe, she could finish high school and get some form of education, and maybe—just maybe—she'd get the chance for a better life.

Jodi did not allow herself to even hope. Numb and resigned to whatever would happen next, Jodi turned from the squad car and stood very still with her hands behind her back. She winced as the cuffs bit into her wrists and took a deep breath as they emptied her pockets. Her lifeline was gone. Then her head was guided into the back of the car ... the warmth of it kissing her skin.

CHAPTER 9

The car skidded on the ice, abruptly startling Sheldon into the present. Steering out of the skid, his heart pounding and his chest filling with panic, Sheldon pulled over to the side of the road, put the car in park and tried to control his breathing.

Once the initial panic subsided, and he managed to get his breathing under control, he started to scan his surroundings. Sheldon had no idea where he was. He glanced at the glowing green light of the clock and realized it was three a.m. He was momentarily relieved. Father would still be passed out drunk in his chair.

There was no way to pull the wool over Father's eyes. A drunkard he might be, but he was no fool. Sheldon knew he would pay dearly for taking the car, unless of course, Father finally died in his sleep.

He knew it was a waste of time at this point to even try to cover this up. *Maybe I'll get lucky. Doubt it though.*

Things had been getting a little easier with Father lately. He seemed to be passed out drunk more often than awake these days, and it had been a while since Sheldon had gotten

a good beating. He did not want one either.

Sheldon took another deep breath. He still could not shake Penny from his mind. He had tried to go for a drive to clear his head but must have lost himself in the pain, as he had no memory of the events that led him here. Sheldon turned off the ignition, and the old car cooled almost immediately. Soon, misty, fleeting clouds plumed with each breath, and condensation started to build up on the windows.

CHAPTER 10

The cops drove her in silence. No one spoke, which was just as well. Jodi wasn't in a mood to talk to them anyway. She had no trust in the cops for good reason, and these were both large, intimidating men. The car was scented with their aftershave intermingled with the smell of leather from the seats. Their uniforms creaked as they shifted beneath the weight of their vests, gun belts, and of course, their night sticks. On more than one occasion, Jodi had seen them beat Indigenous and other minority men to a bloody pulp for even a minor indiscretion, or more likely, for no reason at all.

For the Indigenous men especially, being beaten was the preferable option to being "arrested" and never seen again. There would be no record of any arrest—not worth the resources or time when they had more important things to deal with, like the welfare of pet dogs locked inside hot cars.

The radio squelched and buzzed in the background. The cold long forgotten, Jodi's relief was slowly turning towards uncertainty and fear. The cops' utter silence was starting to feel eerie. They had not told her why she was picked up,

had not even asked her name, and hadn't called in to the station to let anyone know that they had her. Nothing. The once peaceful silence was now maddening, making each second feel like an hour, and anxiety started to build in her chest, quickening her heartbeat and squeezing off her oxygen supply. Something was not right. She looked into the rear-view mirror and saw the cold eyes of the cop in the driver's seat staring back at her.

She hastily looked away, watching as the city lights began to fade behind her, engulfing the car in darkness. The only lights visible were those of the headlights cutting through the fog ahead.

Finally, she could hold back no longer. "Where are you taking me?"

They responded to her question with the same icy silence. She started to panic now, a list of all the missing women she knew running through her head. All of them having just disappeared unexpectedly. It was happening more often lately. One woman would be gone, and another would fill their place. It was possible that they had each been picked up for prostitution or petty crimes, but the police should not have been able to hold them for too long before releasing them back onto the streets. The sheer number of disappearances could hardly be explained by various stints in prison.

The cops didn't bother with them too much anyway, other than a few arrests here and there to meet their quotas. Prostitutes were easy pickings on an otherwise slow night. Cockroaches that just could not be exterminated, and they

usually had bigger fish to fry.

And anyway, life on the street was nomadic. People came and went. No one really gave it too much thought, especially if they were new to the streets or just passing through. They were all aware that they were just a cold case waiting to happen—the hooker, the filthy homeless drunk, the ranters, and the ravers. They moved on, they overdosed, or they died. Their disappearances were just looked at as an occupational hazard, especially for a police force busy looking for misplaced housewives who were late for dinner.

Jodi's anxiety grew and as they drove deeper and deeper into no man's land. She had absolutely no idea where they were and had seen nothing but snow, trees, and darkness for quite a while now as the car continued its journey. The cop in the passenger seat opened his window, letting cold air fill the car as he lit a smoke and inhaled deeply. Jodi watched as he poured out her coke onto the dash of the car and took a bump.

At that moment, the pit of her stomach filled with ice. She knew these cops did not fall into the "serve and protect" category. She heard her SIM card snap, and she watched as the cop threw his cigarette and her phone out the window. She looked back to see the embers of the cigarette skitter as it hit the ground before it was enveloped in a cloud of snow. The panic attack hit her hard. Pure terror rippled through her body, and she clawed at her throat trying to breathe.

They kept driving for what felt like forever before finally stopping. In front of them was a narrow trail that looked like

it might have been cut between trees by a pair of snowshoes. It was hard to say for certain, as the tracks were covered by the additional snow that had fallen since they'd been made.

No fresh ones. Not good.

Jodi knew that *nothing* good was going to happen. Nothing ever did really. That was the life of a sex worker. She hadn't told Larry, Sheila, or even the nurses what had sent her to the hospital those weeks ago, and doubted they'd believe her if she did. But there was not a woman on the street that had not been raped, beaten, or robbed repeatedly. It always felt like she barely survived one incident before being thrown right into another, sometimes with barely any time passing in between.

Her body did not have much desire for life left, but that still did nothing to quell her utter fear. Terror still tore through her as the cop in the passenger seat got out and opened her door.

The other cop got out now, and together, they pulled her to her feet, turning her around and pushing her up against the cop car.

Jodi could feel hot breath on her neck. She was no stranger to what would happen now. They would rape her and then drop her back off where they had found her, knowing she couldn't and wouldn't report them.

Even if I did, who is going to believe a junkie whore making accusations against two respected police officers?

Jodi prayed it was quick. This would likely be her last ride. She didn't think her body could live through another

rape. She was about to explain this to the officers and ask if there was any other way that she could please them, but then thought twice. If she told them her weakness, it would make things even worse. She finally accepted that she didn't have any control over the situation and just surrendered to it.

Jodi adopted the position, the ice-cold wind blowing through her skirt as she waited for the sound of their belts being unbuckled. What she heard first was the click of the handcuffs, and then felt an odd lightness in her arms and shoulders as the blood began circulating again. To her surprise, her skirt stayed where it was, and after a moment, it seemed their belts would as well. She was skeptical and wary. If this wasn't about sex, then what were they doing in the middle of nowhere? She heard the cops walk away from her then, followed by the slam of car doors as they got back inside. The passenger-side window rolled down, and the cop whistled her over to it. She hesitated and then walked slowly towards him.

"Come on," the cop said, smiling. "Come over here. I'm not going to bite. Just come here."

She saw that he was in a jovial mood, his eyes filled with mirth. When she reached the side of his car, he held out her lighter, her smokes, and her whiskey. She took them cautiously, still trying to wrap her head around this strange turn of events.

"Welcome to the Starlight Express!" he said then. "We hope you enjoyed your ride and don't forget to recommend us to all your friends."

With that, they howled with laughter, the driver slammed his foot on the accelerator, and they peeled away, spraying her with cold, powdery snow.

Jodi stood there completely still and utterly stunned. *What the fuck?* She watched as their brake lights were swallowed by the still and silent night. *Great joke*, she thought, waiting anxiously for their return. It wasn't long before she realized they really weren't coming back.

"Oh my god! They really left me here," she said in utter disbelief. "They left me here to die." She looked up into the night sky ... at the innumerable stars that pierced the darkness. *The Starlight Express.*

Under any other circumstances, the sky above her would have entranced her with its surreal beauty, but not tonight. She was nowhere near civilization, she had no phone, and her outfit was nowhere near warm enough to protect her from the cold until she could get to safety. She'd survived earlier, of course, as cold as she'd been, but as the night had deepened, the temperature had plummeted. She could feel the air stinging even her throat and lungs now. She would be lucky if she made it a half hour.

She stood there motionless for a long time, watching the stars at first and then the darkness into which the car had disappeared, still unable to comprehend that she had been unceremoniously abandoned like this—although she was surprised that it had even surprised her. It seemed a fitting end somehow. This was to be the very last miserable chapter of her life. Then the story would finally be over. Some time,

maybe days later—or not until the spring—her frozen body would be found. Just another junkie prostitute who had overdosed and died of hypothermia. No one would miss her or shed a tear.

What did it matter anyway? What was her life besides sadness, pain, and suffering?

As the cold crept in so deep that it started to feel warm on her skin, she began to welcome her death and felt relief wash over her. *It's finally over...* She chugged the three small bottles of whiskey and enjoyed the heat as it burned its way down into her stomach. *A fitting last meal.* She laughed then and lit a cigarette. Careful not to let it fall from her numb fingers, she tried to enjoy it as much as she could, inhaling deep and letting it out slow. It was the last one she would ever have.

As the booze started going to her head, she began to feel warm and sleepy and decided to walk across to the other side of the road, where she sat down heavily in a bank of snow. She was just so tired. Getting warmer by the moment, without thinking or even being consciously aware of it, she peeled off her pea coat, then her top, then her boots...

When she was finally comfortable and ready to sleep, she saw a beautiful face, smiling down at her. Reaching out, Jodi stroked her mother's cheek for a moment before letting her hand fall unnoticed to her side once more.

"Sleep, little bird," said a faraway voice. "You are safe, and I love you." She felt a kiss on the top of her head that filled her entire body with warmth that felt like liquid gold. Jodi smiled then, as she let go, giving herself over to the universe.

CHAPTER 11

1 9 7 2

The coughing had worsened as the months went by. Mother was no longer able to get out of bed. Day and night, Jodi had laid with her. For a while, she had made up silly songs, and Mother would laugh, but that had long since stopped. Every laugh now brought spurted clots of blood into the crumpled tissues Mother held to her mouth. She began to sleep more and started to refuse food and water. Her breath was raspy, and her chest made a strange rattle that got louder and more pronounced as the days went by.

No matter how hard Jodi had tried to get Mother to go to the hospital, she would not, as there was no money to spare. Her inhalations had turned to deep wheezes.

"Come here, child," Mother whispered in a voice that was barely audible. She held her hand to Jodi's cheek, the dry leather of her palms caressing the young girl with whatever was left of her strength. "Life will be hard for you, no doubt, and you will suffer. There will be loss and pain. This is your journey, and you must follow it to come full circle."

Crying, Jodi held her hand and kissed the tops of her knuckles.

"I'm scared, Mother. Please, don't leave me."

"I will never leave you, little dove. I will always be watching you and guiding you. Even when you think I could not possibly be there, I am. Hold your head high and carry on. I love you...." Mother quieted then and would no longer move or open her eyes. The wheezes had stopped.

Jodi needed to get help, and she needed to do it now. She covered Mother with as many blankets as she could find and tucked her in tight before turning on the lamp for her, in case she woke up at night and could not see. She lit a large fire to keep her warm, and put water and blueberry preserves in a bowl on the side of the bed, so that she would have something to eat and drink.

Once when she had been little, maybe three or four, she had fallen and broken her arm. Mother had placed her arm in a sling, so it did not move or jostle, and had put her in a sled, pulling her for what felt like hours until she had reached the trapper's house. The trapper had taken them to a hospital, on his ATV, and a nice man had set her arm in a cast. When they had finished, the trapper had given them a ride home.

Jodi needed to find him now. She remembered her mother pulling her in the sled, although she didn't really remember which way they'd gone, only that the trek had seemed to take forever. Of course, she'd been very little at the time, so maybe it hadn't taken as long as it had seemed. She hoped not. She needed to do her best to find him so that he could help save Mother.

She found the sled out back in the small shed, dragged it to the house, and loaded it with preserves, some fresh bread, and a thermos of water. Scanning the house and deciding that there

wasn't too much more she needed, she looked in on Mother one more time. Blood had dribbled down onto her chin. Jodi scrambled to leave. She had to get help immediately!

Jodi donned her furs, grabbed the snowshoes off the wall, and with one last look, she left her house. Outside, she saw that there were skidoo trails going in both directions. She had a choice to make, left or right, and she had absolutely no idea which way she should go. She started to cry. Mother would die if she picked the wrong trail. It was also entirely possible that she could get lost and never find her way back. She looked at each trail again, walking them both a few hundred meters, as she tried to decide. Looking down the path to the left, she saw fresh wolf prints. She walked back down the right trail and saw none. She decided to walk the path of the sacred wolf. She was sure this was the path she must take and prayed she would get to the house in enough time to save Mother. She started off fresh, strong, and determined.

Jodi knew she could not stop, Mother's life depended on it. What water she had managed to conserve was soon frozen, along with the preserves. The fresh bread was long gone. She had nothing to light a fire with and did not have the energy to try. There was no shelter along her path, and there was nowhere she could stop to ward off the freezing wind. She had sweat through her under layers from the challenge of breaking ground and pulling the sled. She tried to strip down, and even removed her sweater entirely, leaving it on the ground in the hopes that she could keep her coat dry, but it was a futile effort. Sweat had already frozen to the inside of her coat, and her body was starting to violently shiver.

Her socks had slipped down, bunching up inside her boots, and her feet were sore and blistered from walking on them. She had long left the sled behind; there was nothing in it that was of any use to her now. She was breaking through snow as deep as her thighs and losing energy fast. She stopped several times, gasping for air. Jodi desperately wanted to give up; she was tired and wanted to sleep. Every time she had those thoughts though, she would remember rocking with Mother in front of the hearth, listening to her hum while she braided Jodi's hair.

Jodi stumbled and fell as hours turned to days. Dawn turned into dusk and dusk into dawn until they slowly blended, until she was no longer aware of time or even herself. She dreamt of wolves running, stars falling, and Mother. Her chills had stopped completely by this time, and heat was rising in her body. She was nodding off, and the cocoon of sleep was threatening to derail her mission.

She slept, she awoke, she crawled, she dreamt. Finally, she surrendered to it. Somehow, Jodi knew Mother was gone, so she could let go now and join her. Just before she gave over to it, she heard a vehicle nearby. Then another. She looked up and saw that the trail had ended, and there was a road up ahead. With the last bit of energy she had, she crawled on her stomach, using her elbows to slowly propel herself forward, until she collapsed at the road. The last thing she heard before the world went black was a car pulling up beside her.

CHAPTER 12

Sheldon saw a police car coming towards him through his side mirror. He heard the car crunch to a stop a few meters behind his car and huddled down as low as he could, praying that the blinding headlights had not given away his presence in the front seat.

To the passersby, the car looked completely abandoned or broken down, left on the side road while its owners had gone for assistance. The car had long-since cooled, and the windows were covered in frost. His heart started to pound as he heard the car door slam and a person crunching through the snow towards him. He heard the chatter of voices through what he thought was a radio, and then he saw a flashlight beaming through the window. Panic ensued. They would find him: a young man with scared eyes driving a vehicle not registered to him. Terror filled his veins, not at being discovered, arrested, or charged, but at having the cop call his father. He put his hand on the ignition and got ready to gun it, but then he heard the cop behind the car yell out, "JG 1127."

A male's voice a little further away shouted back, "It belongs

to that piss-pot Frank! We're good! Nothing to worry about." The closer cop turned back towards his squad car and started to walk away.

"Haven't seen him in the drunk tank in quite a while," the other cop said. "Bet he drove here completely loaded, stumbled out there into the woods, drunk as shit, and died in the snow."

"Did you want me to call it in?"

"God, no! Think I wanna go searching for him in this weather? Or deal with the paperwork? Or bring attention to that bitch? We were never here."

Sheldon breathed a huge sigh of relief as he heard the man get back in the cop car, slam the door, and then the car driving away. He waited until the taillights disappeared before starting the car; he was frozen. He sat there for a while, absorbing the heat as it kicked in. His heart had finally slowed, and he was starting to be able to think straight. He still wasn't sure where he was, so he nestled back in the seat and thought about which way would get him back home to whatever punishment was waiting for him.

Finally, he decided to turn around and go back in the direction the cops had come from. The last thing he needed was to catch up to them. After driving for a few minutes, over slippery, bumpy roads, he became aware of the heavy fullness of his bladder and knew that he wouldn't make it too much farther.

"Dammit," he mumbled to himself. He didn't want to go out into the cold. He looked for a good spot to park, cranked

up the heat, soaked in as much warmth as his body could. He opened his car door, went around the back of the car, unzipped his pants, and felt the intense relief as he melted the snow in front of him. The cold was cruel, and his stream seemed unending. Once finished, he headed eagerly back to the car when he heard something rustling to the left of him, and then the high-pitched screech of a bird.

The sound pierced the silence, sounding remarkably close. He turned towards it just in time to see an eagle take flight and soar above him, its silhouette becoming one with the moon and the stars. He had never seen one in real life and forgot all about the cold for a moment, mesmerized by the sight and stunned by its beauty and how majestic it was. He watched as it soared upward, shaking his head, and wondering what in the world it was doing in the area at all. Then he heard a whimper from the snow up ahead, breaking his reverie and he looked for its source. Within a few steps, it came into view. Lying in the snow was the body of a naked woman. Her clothes were strewn all around her, and her long dark braid was frosted white. Rushing forward, he crouched down and laid a hand to her cold chest, not releasing his held breath until he felt her heart beating faintly under the palm of his hand and saw the faintest wisp of breath rise from her open mouth. She was alive and hanging on, though barely.

Sheldon scooped her up and cradled her to his chest, startled by how light and frail she seemed.

After a moment of struggle, he managed to get the back door open and laid her gently on the seat of the car. He

wrapped her into the blanket on the back seat. Ensuring that the heat was still cranked up to maximum, Sheldon stripped down to his underwear then and lay down next to her, wrapping them both in the blanket, gladly accepting her cold as he gave to her his heat. He talked softly to her, reassuring her, and hoping she would wake up. He studied her closely. Just like his face, hers bore the scars of a hard life ... but she was beautiful. He kissed her gently on the cheek, and then rested his head against hers. For the next few hours, he stayed with her like that, just waiting for her body to warm and for her heartbeat to get stronger. A soft smile graced his face as his heart expanded with warmth and tenderness.

Sheldon had been watching her all night and had noticed the track marks on her arms, the scabs and scars on her beautiful face, and the gauntness in her cheeks. He'd also taken note of the clothes he had gathered from the snow around her. It wasn't hard to piece together that she was a prostitute, as well as an intravenous drug user, or to conclude that some very cruel, very callous person had left her to die after they'd gotten what they'd wanted from her. Her life no longer seemed in imminent danger. She was warm now, there was a flush of colour in her cheeks, and her heartbeat had grown stronger.

Seeing the newness of her track marks though, he knew there would soon be another threat to contend with. As weak as she clearly was, she would need drugs, or the withdrawal could kill her. Getting quickly dressed, Sheldon tucked her tightly into the blanket and climbed into the front seat, pulled

out, and followed the road the cops had taken...hoping it led him to downtown, to the strip.

He pulled up to the corner and rolled the window down. A beautiful queen came up to his car and bent down low to look at him through the window.

"Hey, honey. What you want?" she asked coyly, giving him a sexy look with insinuating eyes.

"Get in," Sheldon said.

The woman walked around the car and slid into the passenger-side door. "Forty for head, a hundred for sex. Though you can have it for fifty, if you take me somewhere nice."

"You're very beautiful," he told her. "And I'll pay you well for your discretion and your help, but I don't need sex." Curious, she looked at him and raised an already arched eyebrow. Not sure how to explain, Sheldon twisted his body to access the back seat and pulled the blanket back, revealing the girl.

"Oh HELL, NO!" she said, her long fingernails grabbing the door handle.

"No! No, it's not what it looks like! I promise. Just please let me explain."

Hearing the sincerity in his young voice, she paused, looking at him, though she kept one hand on the door handle at the ready.

"Listen, I found her dumped out in the back forty, barely alive. She was hypothermic, so I warmed her up as best as I

could, and I'm going to take her somewhere safe so she can heal. I can tell she injects drugs though, and I don't know how to take care of that, so the withdrawal doesn't kill her. I just … I just need to know what she uses, and how much to give her to avoid making things worse! I also need to buy whatever she is taking. I will make it worth your time. I promise."

The woman looked into his eyes for a long moment. He was young and did seem sincere and compassionate.

"Please, miss? I swear I just want to help her."

She sighed, and felt her shoulders relax slightly. One of those Good Samaritan, bible thumpers always trying to save people and lead them to the light. Either way, money was money. She reached back and took the girl's arm, looking at it for a few seconds.

"Hold on, honey," she said, opening the car door. "I'll get you what you need."

She came back a few minutes later with the dope, and explained how he had to prepare it, and how to inject it. She told him to start with an exceedingly small dose when he got to wherever they were going and to repeat it on a regular basis. "Don't forget, only a very small dose. I don't know how much she uses, so it's best to play it safe so you don't OD her."

"Thank you! Thank you so much," he said, stuffing a wad of cash into her hand and hoping it was enough. He was momentarily grateful that he had cashed his cheque from work earlier that day. By the look in her eyes, he could tell that it was. She seemed in a hurry to get out of the car, as though she were afraid he would change his mind and ask for it back.

As she got out, he leaned towards her. "I might need more drugs, depending on how this goes."

"Name's Rhonda, and I'm here every night, sugar. If I ain't, wait out, and I'll be back soon. Now, honey, don't *you* never try that shit, okay? It's poison."

With that, she stuffed the cash into her bra, wished him luck, and sashayed her beautiful body back to the others.

Sheldon drove home and parked the car, leaving her where she was for now as he walked inside to make sure Father was passed out in his chair as usual. He was, so he returned to the car, lifting her carefully out of the back seat, and took her inside, carrying her quietly past Father. He knew that, if it came to it, he would protect her from him at all costs, but he hoped he wouldn't have to. He had a plan, though not much of one. Still, it should work at least until she was back on her feet.

He placed the still unconscious woman gently on the bed in the basement, then retrieved the small black bag that Rhonda had given him, prepared the dope as instructed, and injected her with a small dose. Finally, hoping desperately that he had done the right thing, Sheldon padlocked the door, making a mental note to get new locks for both the room and the basement door. Fear was racing in his heart, but he tried to stay calm. It wasn't like Father ever came down here anymore, but he would take every precaution. No one was going to harm her anymore. Not on his watch.

Once Sheldon was sure she was settled, he crept back up the stairs and quietly locked the basement doors.

CHAPTER 13

Jodi's cheeks, fingers, and thighs burned. Her mouth was dry, and her lips were chapped. Swallowing was excruciating. She tried to open her eyes, but her lids were too heavy. Instead of darkness though there was a warm pink glow shining through them. The eyes beneath felt dry and full of sand. There was a comfortable bed beneath her though, and soft sheets cocooning her tightly. She also felt the warmth of a man beside her, holding her to his chest and lightly stroking her hair. Too tired and comfortable to be scared, she snuggled into his safety and comfort.

The smell of flowers scented the air. Paired with the fact that a man was beside her, holding her tight, she assumed that she was either in a pleasant hotel or the John's home. A rare treat. Apparently, he had actually allowed her to stay with him and spend the night.

Not all Johns were cruel and depraved. Once in a blue moon, she got to experience this gloriousness. Usually, the John was an awkward virgin trying to learn and still innocent enough to romanticize the experience. There were also lonely,

caring souls just looking for comfort. It didn't balance the scale of suffering she'd endured but was usually enough to put a bandage over her bullet holes.

She felt a small needle prick and faded back into unconsciousness. As she slipped into the comforting darkness, she could hear the steady beating of drums and a beautiful melody. The sound stirred inside her a long-lost sense of pride and deep sorrow.

Jodi woke up to a freight train running through her head. She was confused and disoriented and had no idea where she was. She remembered waking up in bed with a John last night and turned over to see him still there. She sat up fast, scanning her surroundings and realized that she wasn't in a hotel room. She was in some sort of showroom, behind a clear Plexiglass wall.

"Where am I? What's going on?" She was bewildered and panic started to set in. She jumped out of the bed, ran for the door, and started pounding on it, yelling for help.

Startled awake, Sheldon quickly leapt out of bed. "No! It's okay!" he said, as soothingly as he could. He approached her slowly with his hands open in front of him. "You're safe. I promise..."

Jodi's back was against the wall now, her terrified eyes scanning the room for anything she could use as a weapon to defend herself.

"Listen, I am not going to hurt you. I *promise* you that you're safe. My name is Sheldon...." His voice was awkward and trembling, which drew her eyes back towards him. He looked

surprisingly young—early twenties maybe—and seemed just as frightened of her as she was of him. He kept glancing nervously at her and then up at the ceiling. "I ... I found you last night, lying in a snowbank. You were barely breathing."

Jodi was immediately assaulted by memories of the night before. She remembered being picked up by the cops, the long silent drive, and laying in the snowbank resigned to her death. Her hand flew to her mouth to stifle a gasp.

"I didn't know you were there, and I was about to drive away, and then I heard you," Sheldon continued, his sentences almost running together in his nervousness. "I put you in the car and laid with you until you were warm. I saw the track marks on your arms, and I knew you would need a fix when you woke up so you wouldn't get sick. I have been giving you little doses throughout the night. I was afraid to wake you. I didn't want to scare you, but it's been a long time since you've had food or water...."

She could feel tears start to prickle the corners of her eyes, realizing that no matter why she was here, this man had saved her from certain death. She looked more closely at him. He was handsome in an odd way, but his body wore a cape of poorly cloaked fear.

"Where am I?" she asked again.

"Don't worry, you're safe—"

"But I'm locked in here," she said, cutting him off, needing more of an answer than that.

"I know how it looks, but you're locked in here for *your* safety. I swear."

"What is this place? And to keep me safe from what?"

"My father is a miniaturist. This is a dollhouse, you know? Like a large-scale model. All I know is that you're safe inside here, and you must stay until I find a way to get you out. I just didn't have anywhere else to bring you. And I'm protecting you from someone who needs to be locked out," he said, his face indicating just how scared he really was.

She considered this. Good Samaritans didn't usually lock people up; they just drive them to the hospital or a shelter maybe. She wanted to trust his motives, despite this, but this room was eerie and strange. Her senses were on high alert, tingling, as if they detected something sinister in the air. Sheldon's explanation seemed plausible, but it just didn't feel right. Yet, he appeared to be sincere, and she could tell he was afraid.

Is he schizophrenic or something? Dissociative identity disorder maybe? He seemed legitimately worried that someone would hurt her, and judging by his darting upward glances, it seemed he thought that person was upstairs. Either way, there had definitely been a little girl kept here, either real or imagined, and neither one of those options comforted her.

"Can I ask you your name?" he asked her nervously, not meeting her eyes.

She looked at him, hesitating, but decided that telling him couldn't hurt anything. Finally, she said, "My name is Jodi."

"Jodi," he said, seeming to turn it over in his head for a moment. "You don't look like a Jodi." They locked eyes then, and his face flamed red. "I-I'm sorry. Jodi is a b-beautiful

name," he stammered.

Something about what he said caused a reaction inside her. A feeling she couldn't quite remember, and a memory she couldn't quite grasp.

"Please, you must eat," he said then, urging her towards a small table, upon which sat a bowl of blueberries and cream. "You must be unbelievably exhausted and hungry," he said, his voice gentle and full of compassion. "I'll give you some dope, if you eat," he said, pulling out a little black bag from a drawer in the nightstand and holding it up.

Staring at it, her heart quickened a beat. No matter how scared she was, the dope prevailed. She thought it out rationally and tried to look at the situation in the best possible light. It wasn't as if this was a trap house ... or the back of a car, she shuddered. She couldn't deny that he had saved her. She had been through hell a thousand times, and no matter what was going on here, she had to have faith that there was a reason for it.

Ultimately, it was what it was. Her only option was to play it cool, stay alert, and plan her escape. With a deep breath, she resigned herself to the situation, ready to accept her fate. Sheldon set the berries in front of her, and she had to admit she was ravenous—for the berries and for the dope that would hopefully follow.

As Jodi bit into the sweet crispness of the berries, a flashback hit her with such force that it made her gasp......

As Mother hunched over the blueberry patch, Jodi twirled around in circles, lost in giggles as she saw millions of berries

all around. Dizzy, she fell in a heap and looked up at the clear blue sky. She flopped over on her tummy then, resting her chin in her hands and watching Mother's nimble fingers quickly and efficiently remove the plump berries from the bush. Mother sorted the berries in her hands by feel, discarding the white ones as well as the mushy ones, filling her second large wicker basket to the brim.

Jodi looked down at her own basket, a few small and misshapen berries rolling around in its bottom. She had eaten more than she had picked, so many that her tummy was sore. Whatever berries she had been able to save from her mouth had spilled, either in her stumbling or when she would knock the basket over while distracted. This had happened so many times that the joy and excitement of picking them had long faded. She rolled onto her back and put her arm over her eyes to shade them from the sun, breathing in the fruit-scented breeze and feeling the sun gently warm her face and toes.

"Your bucket is empty," said Mother.

"I keep spilling them all, so I gave up. There's no point," she said in a whiney voice and then sighed.

Mother softly pinched her fingers on Jodi's chin, cradling it in her hand. "Nothing is ever a waste of time, dovey. All is time well spent. You practise, you learn, you fall, and you grow."

"Well, I don't see how spilling a hundred buckets of blueberries on the ground is not a waste of time," she huffed. "I'm bored."

"Well, the berries you dropped will feed the baby birds and their mothers, the scurrying little field mouse, and all the tiny little ants. Whatever doesn't fill the tummies of your little

friends will go back to the loving arms of Mother Earth, so she can replenish and give to you again and again. It is all a circle, little bird, and you are a part of that. If you hadn't dropped the berries, how many animals wouldn't have had their supper?" Mother laughed at her and stuffed a handful of berries into her mouth, making her cheeks bulge. Purple juice flowed down over her wrinkled chin as she giggled. When she laughed, she sounded like a young girl, and Jodi could see the youth in her mother's face. She could almost imagine what she'd looked like when she was little.

"Now, get your little rump over her, and I will show you how. It won't be easy, but the good things in life seldom are." Mother put her lips close to her ear then, her warm breath tickling Jodi's face. "You want to know a secret? The pain you feel is necessary, and you need to harness it and learn to ride its course. If it wasn't for that pain, the berry would never be as sweet on your tongue."

Mother winked at her and cuddled her close then from behind, kissing her head, and placing the empty basket firmly between her legs. "Pick as many as you can before moving on. Keep your hand loose and roll the berries gently from your fingers into the bucket. Don't worry about the bad ones, the white ones, the bugs, or the sticks; it'll all come out in the wash. The more you do it, the faster and easier it will become. That isn't going to happen today, so get that out of your head. Free your mind of negative emotions and thoughts, like 'I can't' and 'this will never work.' Focus on each little berry, feel the sun, smell the wind, listen to the cicadas' hum, and the birds chirp while you fill your bucket. If something grumpy pops into your beautiful head, change it to be grateful for

Mother Earth's gifts all around us. You go ahead and try it now."

Mother moved on to the next bush, humming the most beautiful melodies as she went. When Jodi's basket was full, she ran over to see her, and tripped right in front of her, spilling the berries again.

Mother really started to laugh now. "Well, my little bird, the mice will have a big dinner party tonight!" They laughed and laughed until Mother started coughing. Once she was able to get the cough back under control, she smiled. "Well, you fell, and its time to get back up and try again! But you need to know when its time to take a deep breath and give your heart and body a little break. It is getting late, and my back is sore. Let's head home…. I will carry the baskets." She laughed again, bringing on a new fit of coughing.

Mother pounded on her chest, clearing her lungs, and spat out that which had been stuck in there. As they descended the blueberry patch headed for home, morbid curiosity made Jodi want to look at the glob left behind. She didn't want to—it made her tummy flip-flop in disgust just thinking about it—but despite this, she couldn't fight the compulsion to look. With a grimace, she looked down at the rock and saw that the glob was chunky and bloody. Almost like the liver Mother would fry up sometimes. Entranced and disgusted, she stared at it for a long time. Then she shuddered and ran to catch up with mother.

Once at home, the picture disappeared from her head as she helped Mother clean the berries. She was excited to have blueberry jam. She spent the rest of the evening listening to her mother spin tales while watching the sun bloom orange and pink in the

window behind her. She loved the setting of the sun, except for the fact that it meant bedtime.

When Jodi finished the last bite, she put her head down in her hands and cried.

"Are you alright?" Sheldon asked.

"Yes," she replied tearfully.

"Would you like your medicine?"

She looked up at him, tears running down her cheeks. "Yes, please," she answered, sad and defeated. She had been unable to shake the memory of Mother's face.

He put out his hand, and she hesitantly took it, allowing him to pull her up from her chair and lead her to the bed. He pulled down the covers for her, and exhausted, she crawled in. She smiled at him gratefully, as he tucked her in and gave her the drugs. She was asleep in seconds.

Sheldon knew he should probably leave her, but he wanted to stay. He went back and forth about what he should do. It would be the appropriate thing to just let her sleep, but he decided that it couldn't hurt to lay down with her.

The next morning, Sheldon awoke early, worried that she'd find him sleeping next to her and be frightened again. She was so beautiful. Dark skin on white sheets. A long black braid draping over her shoulder. He had wanted to touch her back ever so gently, and kiss all the little scars there, but had decided that lying there beside her was enough, and that touching her without asking would not be the right thing to do. He wanted to go get Jodi a few things. So, he made her a nice breakfast and then left her a note.

CHAPTER 14

Father was nowhere to be seen, which meant he had gone to the pub and would be drinking all day and night. There was no way he'd be home until this evening. If he was gone past lunch, that meant he'd started drinking on awakening and wouldn't be home at all today. This could go on with Father for days, weeks even. He didn't want to leave Jodi there alone, but he felt safe knowing that Father hadn't gone down into that basement once in the last fifteen years.

When Sheldon was younger, he had taken to going down in the basement when Father was gone, unlocking the doors with keys that Father had never noticed he had stolen. He would go down there often to lay on the bed and smell the scent of roses in the air. The room made him feel happy. He would bring down the little yellow blanket from his closet with him. He always wondered if the blanket and the room had belonged to the same person. They smelled the same. He would never dare ask Father about the room though. It sort of looked like one of those show-room bedrooms you see in stores. Father had left it locked up tight. It was surely one of Father's projects. He made stuff like that all the

time. Once he had even made Sheldon a little mountain diorama, with a train that moved! He had loved that gift so much, but like most things he loved, Father destroyed it.

Once, when Sheldon had been around six years old, Father had left him alone for a few days. He loved being alone during the days, but he was scared at night. The house was dark and made spooky, creaky sounds, raising the hair on his arms. He didn't have a nightlight because Father said that they were for babies. Usually, the dark didn't scare him because he knew that Father was at home at least. As much as he enjoyed the days alone without Father, he had to admit there was some type of security with him there at night.

That night was really scary, the scariest one so far. The wind was howling outside, and the shutters banged. He could hear a pack of coyotes yipping, and it sounded as if they were right in the backyard. He was sure they were going to come in and eat him. His anxiety grew and festered as his mind went wild with monsters. Finally, unable to quell the fear, he ran to the closet and pulled out the yellow blanket. He pulled it over himself and letting the soft fabric and relaxing smell float over him. It wasn't long before he'd fallen asleep, awakening only when his body had hit the floor. Hard.

When he'd looked up, Father had been standing over him, shaking the blanket in his face. "WHERE DID YOU GET THIS?" he'd screamed with boozy breath. Spittle had flown from his mouth with the force of his anger, and Sheldon had cowered, waiting to be punched.

"You tell me where you got this, and you tell me right now!"

"I f-found it in the c-closet," Sheldon had stammered, still waiting for the blows to start raining down. He always hated waiting for it, and just wanted it to be over with. When a few minutes had passed, he braved a peek and saw Father standing there frozen, holding the blanket in his hand, staring at it. Finally, he threw the blanket at Sheldon, with tears in his eyes. He had never seen Father cry.

"Don't let me ever see that fucking thing again or I'll burn it," he said as he stormed out of the room, with Sheldon staring after him in shock. He took the blanket and hid it back in the closet. It was never talked about again.

CHAPTER 15

1991

She still haunted Frank's dreams every night. He would be watching her in the room, waiting for her to turn and take off her nightgown. When she turned around though, her nightgown was falling off her body in ribbons, and there was a dead baby hanging from her by its umbilical cord. Her face was moldy, and her teeth were black. Her eyes were cloudy, and chunks of her cheeks were falling off. The hair on her head was patchy or missing in places, except for two stringy pigtails, tied with ribbons. She'd point at him with a bony finger, the fingernail hanging off. After seeing her in the basement room one time too many, he had locked it up and had never gone down there again. Not that it mattered. She always followed him, showing up in places even when he was awake. He'd taken to drinking himself to a stupor most days, so he didn't have to face her anymore.

That night, Frank had woken up on his own with no dreams of her, relatively functional and with the hunger for violence grumbling inside him. It had been a long time since

he had enacted his sadistic fantasies and he'd known exactly what he'd wanted. Downing the last quarter of his sixty, he'd gotten ready fast, excited for the night.

Frank had been cruising up and down the street for hours now, watching and waiting. He didn't like to pick up when there were a lot of hookers milling around, not wanting to bring attention to himself or his car. It had been a few weeks since he'd last hunted, and there was no way that she had lived through it. Frank had watched the news, but as always, there was nothing about some missing hooker, living or dead. He laughed. There never would be. No one ever looked for them. He could pick them off by the hundreds and no one would even bat an eye. His violence grew more brutal each time, and it was taking more and more to satisfy his sadistic urges.

He spotted her then. She looked young, just how he liked them. She was petite, olive-skinned.... She would do. Judging by the look of her, she would not be missed, and she definitely was too weak to fight him. He was going to have fun with this one. Make it last, inflict violence on her gradually, keep her alive as long as possible. He circled the block one more time, waiting for her to make it to the darker, quieter part of the strip.

Frank rolled the stop as he was turning around the corner and saw a flash of blue and red lights whirling behind him. "Fuck," he spat. He gathered his documents together and waited for the officer to approach.

"Licence and registration," the officer said curtly.

Goddamn it! This was no rookie, and he knew he wasn't

going to be able to sweet talk his way out of this one. Oh well, it was just a traffic violation. Take the fine and go. At least he hadn't been caught picking up the hooker. The officer leaned into the driver's window, scanning the car with his flashlight. Frank panicked a little, because he hadn't cleaned out the back of his car after his last two encounters.

"Sir, have you been drinking? I can smell alcohol in the vehicle," the cop asked, staring directly into his eyes.

"Yes, sir, but only a bit. I was just driving home from the bar. I had two drinks of whiskey neat over the past four hours. I was the DD. I just finished taking a few guys from one bar and dropping them off at another; drunk idiots, you know how they are. Lucky, they didn't puke in the car." He chuckled casually.

The cop didn't even crack a smile. "Stay here, sir."

Frank watched the man head back to his vehicle, hoping he had convinced him with his phoney storey, and that he was just gone to fill out a ticket for him. He looked out his rear-view mirror, watching the cop in his car.

A few minutes later, the cop started back toward him and stopped beside his window. "Frank, is it?"

"Yes, sir."

"I just ran your plates, Frank, and it appears this isn't the first time you have been stopped for alcohol-related offences. Breathe into this, please." The cop held out the breathalyzer, and Frank knew he was fucked.

Shit! He blew into the machine, knowing he was going to fail miserably.

After only a moment's consideration of the results, the cop nodded. "Please, step out of the car, Frank. You're under arrest for impaired driving."

Frank did as he was told and was quickly cuffed, walked to the police car, and put in the back seat. *Sheldon!* He thought then with relief. *Sheldon will bail me out.*

After Frank was processed at the county jail, he was thrown into the drunk tank where he waited to receive his first phone call. When he finally got it, he dialed the house phone several times, his blood boiling more and more with each missed call. Finally, Sheldon picked up.

"Why the fuck weren't you answering the phone?!" Frank yelled. His question was met with silence. All he could hear was his son's breathing. *Fuck it.* "Look, I'm at county. I'll get arraigned soon, so pick up my car from the strip before they impound it, get your ass over here, and bail me out." Silence on the other line. "Did you hear me, fucker?"

Sheldon put the phone receiver back on its cradle. Over the next few minutes, the phone rang over and over. He finally disconnected it from of the wall.

Sheldon didn't want Father out on bail. This was his third DUI, so if no one came to bail him out, he would have to stay in jail until his hearing. Sheldon knew he wouldn't be getting away without a stint in jail this time. Either way though, he knew he was safe from him for at least a few days, or maybe weeks.

Fuming, Frank called Marc, his old drinking buddy. *Lord knows I've bailed that piss bag out enough times. He owes me.*

"Yeah? H'lo?" Marc slurred.

"Sober the fuck up. I need you to bail me out of county and bring my car. I'm sure they'll have it impounded by morning."

"I got not money, Frank."

"Well, you better find some," Frank answered in a threatening tone.

There was a prolonged period of silence on the line before Marc gave in. "I got my social security coming next week," he mumbled. "I can bail you out with that, but I got no more now."

"For fuck sakes!" Frank yelled into the phone, before slamming it down. His face was flushed, red and hot, his rage at full boil as he thought of Sheldon. Through gritted teeth, he growled, "He will pay when I get home."

This time he would pay dearly.

CHAPTER 16

Jodi awoke to the smell of coffee and looked over on the table beside her. There was a little pot full of steaming hot coffee, and muffins that were still warm. Her tummy rumbled. There was a note on the table: *"Didn't want to wake you. Just gone out for a little while. I'll be back soon – S."*

Jodi looked around the room again and sighed, remembering where she was. She was upset that she was being held here against her will, but the more she thought about it.... Where exactly was it that she needed to go? She was warm, clean, and dry and her stomach was full. Sheldon was gentle and courteous. He had never once hurt her with words or fists. He didn't even try to touch her, let alone have sex with her. He had saved her from a certain death, and he seemed to be open, trustworthy, and generous. He had been patient with her when she'd woken up in a state of panic, and most importantly, he didn't withhold dope from her. She didn't get near as much as she would like, but the supply was steady, and her cravings didn't overwhelm her as much anymore. She actually did feel safe with him. Under different circumstances, this would have been her dream.

CHAPTER 17

Sheldon had been beyond ecstatic ever since the phone call. Not only was Father in jail but Sheldon had finally been able to stand up for himself. It had felt amazing! This solved so many problems. Jodi was his first priority, and now he didn't need to worry about Father hurting her.

Sheldon revelled in his happiness until he realized that if Father wasn't a threat to her anymore, then he'd have to let her go. He could just lie to her, of course, but that wouldn't feel right. His balloon quickly deflated as he pulled the car he'd retrieved into the driveway. Relieved to have found it before it had been towed to impound, he had taken full advantage, using it to go shopping for Jodi, buying her pajamas, a pair of sweatpants and t-shirts, some undergarments, and socks. He'd also bought her nice smelling bath products, toiletries, and a few books. He carried all the bags from the car into the house, though all the excitement he'd had at the thought of giving them to her had dissipated with the realisation that he had no justification for keeping her there any longer. He unlocked the basement door and headed down to see her,

presents in hand.

Jodi was awake when he got back, looking brighter than she had before. He showed her all the gifts he had purchased for her. First, her expression was one of shock, and then tears brimmed her eyes when she realized they were really for her. "Thank you," she said, holding the pajamas to her face and rubbing the soft fabric on her cheeks. She placed all the other clothing on the desk, along with the books. Then she took all her new bath stuff to the bathroom at the back of the enclosed space, lining up all the pots and potions on the vanity.

"Sheldon, thank you. Thank you for everything," she said, gratitude clear on her face and in her eyes.

Sheldon's heart was breaking. "Jodi, can you come here?"

When she had settled on the edge of the bed near where he stood, he cleared his throat and then began to speak, his voice solemn. "I was keeping you here to keep you safe from my father. He's been brutally abusive all of my life. When I found you, I knew that you needed somewhere to heal, or you would die out there. I took you here to help you get better, knowing that this room was secure. He no longer has the keys, and he would never come down here anyway.... But neither of us need to worry anymore. He called late last night. He's in jail for a DUI, and with his record, he will be for some time. He's not a threat to either of us for now." His voice was choked with sadness.

Sheldon walked over to the door of the plexiglass room. "It's safe now, so you can pack up your things. I'll get you a bag, and I can drop you off wherever you like. I'll get you some

cash to help you out too," he said with a pained expression on his face, as he sighed, and opened the door.

Is he really just going to let me go? Jodi asked herself. She took careful steps towards the door, waiting for him to grab her, but he just held the door open so that she could pass. As she did, her body tensed, waiting for a knife to the back, or a hard shove from behind. Heart racing, she walked towards the basement steps then, and looked up. She saw that the basement door at the top was open. She walked up to the top step and through the doorway, then closed the door behind her, leaning her back against it.

From where she stood, she could see the front door of the house. She could be through it and gone in just a few seconds. *He let me go,* she thought then. *He didn't have to, but he did.* He had saved her, even though he was clearly terrified of his father, and he seemed to genuinely care for her well-being. Sheldon had never stepped over the line, always the perfect gentleman.... She realized then that he really had just meant to keep her safe.

What reason is there to leave? Jodi asked herself then. She dug as deep as she could and couldn't find a single one. She had never felt comfort or care like this, not since she'd lost her mother. She had never even been treated like a human being. Even the kind, gentle Johns she had met in her travels still left her after the evening was over ... with nowhere to go and nothing to eat.

This was everything she had ever wanted, right here, but that room bothered her. Why would his father have built a

life-sized dollhouse, for what reason? If it was a project for work, then why didn't he dismantle it, and why would he lock his son out of there? If his father didn't go down there, why was it there at all? That was the thing that Jodi really couldn't get over. It tainted the situation with distrust, and Jodi couldn't help but wonder if there were an ulterior motive lurking around the corner. She actually didn't want to leave, but she had to know about the room.

Jodi took a big breath, not sure if what she was doing was the right thing and headed back down the stairs. Sheldon looked up at her. He was surprised but assumed she had just returned for her things. He watched as she walked back into the room and sat down beside him on the bed. She took his hand in hers then and was amazed when, trembling, he started to cry.

"Sheldon, I need to know what you know about this room."

Sheldon's face crumpled. He was silent then for a long time. Finally, he took a deep breath, and in a shaky voice he said, "I will tell you all that I know."

1974

Sheldon had wet his bed again, so he had stripped his sheets and quietly padded down the stairs to the kitchen. Father was sleeping in his chair. He wasn't allowed to go down the stairs to the basement for any reason, and there would be hell to pay if he was caught, but he was pretty sure that was where the laundry room would be, and he couldn't bear to have a repeat of what had followed his last bed-wetting incident. Either way, there was the risk of severe punishment.

Perhaps Father would sleep all day like he sometimes did. He could only hope. The basement door was actually open a crack, which it never was. Maybe that was a sign? Taking a deep breath, he held it, listening hard to make sure Father was fully asleep. He seemed to be. Still, he hesitated, feeling stuck and not knowing what he should do. He listened to his father snoring for another long moment, and then with a big brave breath, he started to descend the cold stairs into the basement. He didn't know where the laundry room might be exactly, and frankly, he didn't even know how to use a washing machine, but he had to try. Sheldon had seen them in movies and TV commercials. The ladies always looked so happy when they smelled the clothes that came out of the machines.

Sheldon began to look around beneath the stairs. There was no light, and his eyes weren't yet adjusted to the dark. He felt around, then pulled back his hand back quickly, shaking it with

disgust when he put it through a spider web. Sheldon hated spiders. Billy at school had told him that they could crawl in your ears and make babies in there who would eat your brain. At night, he would always wrap his head in a blanket and crawl into his closet to hide from the spiders, and other things. The closet was Sheldon's little comfy nest. It was warm and cozy and hid his most favourite possession: a soft, yellow, knitted blanket that smelled like roses. Sheldon loved the smell of the blanket. It made him feel loved and warm. He had run his finger over the stitches so many time that he could identify all the little imperfections; where stitches had been dropped and left little holes, or when the loops on the row looked completely different midway. It was what made it special. He had found it one day, hiding behind some old moth-eaten clothes. He had held it to his cheek, smelling it and rubbing it on his face. He didn't dare take the blanket in the closet out and into bed with him though because he was terrified of what would happen if Father knew he had it, and he didn't want to lose it.

Sheldon scanned the entire room but didn't see any machine like the ones on TV. As he searched, he became distracted by a soft pink light emanating from a recessed wall at the very back of the room. Curious, he tiptoed towards it. He rounded the wall and noticed that the light was coming from an open door near the end of the hallway. Fear long forgotten, he followed the pink light into a bedroom and gasped in surprise, dropping his sodden bed sheets on the floor.

The room was cut in half by a very thick, clear wall that almost reached to the ceiling. Inside the plastic, facing him, was a large,

comfy-looking wooden bed painted white, with a pink bedspread and big, comfy, heart-shaped, pink and white pillows. In the middle of the bed was nestled a beautiful little baby doll that wore a pale-pink coat with a hood trimmed in fluffy white fur. The bed had a canopy with sheer curtains that hung down over the bed, tied back on either side by large white bows.

There was a little white dresser, to the left of the bed, with pink handles and several drawers, and a white desk to the right which held a lamp with pink soft light glowing. There was a sparkly pink curtained area that was open somewhat, behind which he could see a large circular tub with a shower attachment and a vanity sink, upon which rested a pink toothbrush and bubble-gum toothpaste. The walls that weren't plastic were painted a pastel purple, bordered in the centre by wallpaper with sparkling, prancing unicorns. Above the border, hung with ribbons, was an odd piece of wood, painted white and stenciled with bears and hearts.

There was also a beautiful Victorian doll house and two hampers. One was filled with yellow wool, which looked oddly familiar. The other hamper was stuffed with plush animals of every variety.

Outside of the room, in front of the plastic wall, was a large rocking chair. There was also a TV attached to a jointed metal arm in front of the chair, apparently so it could be moved and seen from the anywhere in the room. Everything was caked in dust.

Sheldon walked closer and closer to the little room. There was a sliding window that was open slightly, from which the scent of roses wafted from the room. He noticed a large bowl in the

corner of the room filled with dried flowers, cinnamon sticks, brightly covered wood chips, and little wicker balls and guessed correctly that they were the source of the lovely fragrance. He inhaled the scent deeply, letting it fill his soul with warmth and love. To enter the room, there was a thick plastic door with a hole cut into it instead of a doorknob. He wanted more than anything to lie down on the comfy bed and snuggle with all the little bears. He tried to open the door, but it was locked up tight and he couldn't reach the deadbolt.

Sheldon turned from the door—looking for something he could stand on to reach the lock—and there was Father, right in front of him, solid and unmoving, a too familiar wildness in his cold eyes. Before Sheldon could even speak, Father had grabbed his hair and slammed the back of his head into the plastic wall. Sheldon crumpled into a pile on the floor, blood running down his neck and back. Father grabbed the wet sheets in one hand and his hair in the other and pulled him to the stairs. Sheldon tried to keep up, but in his pain and disorientation, he kept falling, his hair being pulled tighter and tighter. Father dragged him back up the stairs, and then down the hall to the bathroom, where he stripped him, placed him naked in the tub, and sprayed him with icy water for what felt like forever.

Sheldon slowly sank to the bottom of the bathtub, under the spray for so long that he no longer felt anything. His toenails and lips were blue, and the violent shivering had stopped. "Get up," demanded Father finally.

Sheldon tried but there was no blood left in his limbs, and he had no feeling in his extremities. Father yanked him out of the

tub and threw him like a ragdoll onto the bathroom floor. The next thing Sheldon remembered was being tightly tucked into bed with a thick quilt.

"You'll be alright," grunted Father, a hint of guilt to his voice.

1991

By now, Jodi could barely hear what Sheldon was saying. He had cried throughout the whole story, and she had cried with him. She could just imagine Sheldon as this tiny little boy, trying to wash his sheets.

"I don't know why this room is here," he said, with stark sincerity. "I never asked. As far as I know, the last time he ever came down here was the day when he found me and almost killed me in the tub. I never stopped being curious about it though. For some reason I can't explain, the room just makes me feel happy. As I got a bit older, I started coming down here when Father was out, and then when he was passed out in his chair as well. I stole his keys, but I don't think he ever even noticed. He never said anything. Somehow, I just knew he would never come down here looking for me again.

When I found you, I thought that I could bring you down here to recover, but I had to make sure Father never found you. Now that he's gone though ... you're safe, and you don't need to stay in here anymore." He rubbed his face roughly, trying to regain his composure.

"Sheldon, I want to stay," she said as she pulled his head into her chest. She held him then and both exhausted they fell asleep in each other's arms.

Sheldon woke her up in the afternoon, and she smiled at him when she opened her eyes.

"Do you want to come with me, Jodi? I want to take you to the doctor. I heard there's some medicine that can help you feel better and manage your cravings. After that, I thought maybe we could go for a drive and have a nice breakfast together, stop at the shops, or maybe go for a walk?"

She laughed. "How about we do them all!"

A large smile broke out on his face. "Sounds good." He held his arms out then, asking for a hug. "May I?"

Jodi responded by snuggling into him and holding him tight, a little smile on her face and a little flutter in her heart as she breathed him in.

"I'm going upstairs to shower and dress. Meet me upstairs at the main door when you're ready?" When she nodded, he continued. "Just turn left at the top of the stairs."

"Got it," she said. She almost skipped to her bathroom. She couldn't remember ever feeling this joyful. She knew that it was time to get some help. She needed to get off the drugs and start an actual life. That said, she hadn't had her fix yet this morning and was feeling it. Sheldon had been giving lower and lower doses each time, but the desire was still there.

She'd have to ask Sheldon for a little more before they went out. She wanted just enough to keep the cravings at bay, but not enough that she couldn't be clear headed and enjoy the day with him. As she cleaned up in the bath, she sang to herself.

Jodi checked herself in the mirror, and she could actually see the difference in her face. Her eyes were sparkling, there was colour in her cheeks, and she was smiling—not a forced

smile either. She was truly smiling. Her skin was clearing up, and overall, she looked and felt much healthier. Jodi did one last check, and then headed up the stairs to meet up with Sheldon, just excited about their day.

When Jodi got to the stop of the stairs, she turned left and started to walk down the hallway. She noticed a decorative pillar wrapped floor to ceiling in a thick brown rope. She put her hand out and very lightly touched the rope, then pulled her hand back immediately, as if it had burned her. Suddenly, she got dizzy and disoriented. She looked down at her feet, and it felt like she was watching them from somewhere outside of her body. Nauseous and faint, her world came to a complete halt. She collapsed forcefully on the ground. Sarah was there. She was hanging from a thick rope, her neck at an odd angle and a puddle of urine on the floor beneath her.

She collapsed.

Sheldon heard a loud thump from the main floor and hurried down the steps to find Jodi lying in a crumpled ball in the hall. She was shaking and sweating, repeating the name "Sarah" repeatedly. Her face was white with shock. He had been giving her less and less dope and worried that he had gone too fast and left her in withdrawal. He needed to get her to a doctor as fast as possible. Sheldon picked her up and carried her to the phone, laying her down gently before grabbing the phone and starting to dial 9-1-1.

"Stop."

Sheldon looked down at her and saw her shaking her head, so he set the phone back in its cradle. "Jodi, what's wrong?"

he asked, his face wrought with worry.

She began sobbing uncontrollably, so he pulled her into his chest and let her cry, soaking his chest with her tears. Jodi kept repeating that same name over and over as she buried herself in his lap and sobbed until she shook. Sheldon's heart broke to see her this way. Finally, she looked up at him with eyes that were red and swollen.

"What's wrong, Jodi? What happened? Who's Sarah? I'm here for you Jodi, I'm here, and you're safe."

She took a deep breath, and after a moment's hesitation, she gave in and let the story spill out of her.

She told him about her mother, about being raised in a residential school. She told him everything that had happened to her while she was there. She told him about Sister Mary and Father Michael, and then without warning she blurted, "They buried Sarah in the schoolyard. They killed her, then just threw her in a hole like garbage," she said, violent shivers running through her as she cried and cried for Sarah.

Taken aback, but trying to remain calm he asked her, "Do you want to tell me about Sarah?"

Jodi looked up at him. Her deep brown eyes and doe-like eyelashes were still beautiful despite the crying. Jodi hesitated; she knew she wanted to tell Sheldon, but just like him, the pain was buried deep inside her, fortified with almost impenetrable walls. Her bottom lip trembled, and tiny tears ran down her cheeks. Her shoulders drooped and her body loosened. Finally, she looked at him, took a deep breath, and gave in, chipping away at the little cracks in her

wall, steadily widening them. "I'm going to need more tissues."

"I'm on it," Sheldon said. "I'll get you some tea with lemon and honey while I'm at it."

When he returned a few minutes later, she was sitting upright, leaning against the wall with her head resting on her knees. Jodi took the mug of tea and held it tightly in her hands, letting the steam warm her face before taking a sip. "Thank you. It's very good."

He passed her the tissues and waited patiently for her to speak. She fumbled at first, visibly uncomfortable and trying to figure out the right place to start, to sort out what information she felt comfortable sharing. Her life felt like a piece of yarn on a sweater. It would take several pulls for it to break free, but once it did, it would quickly unravel. She looked at Sheldon and tried to smile but couldn't. He didn't know much about her life yet. At the root of it all, she knew she had been using the drugs to forget what had happened: the pain, the hurt, the loss of everything important to her. Now, as she had been slowly weaning off the dope, the flashbacks had started to assault her. Dreams of a thousand unwanted memories.

Jodi had never told her story to anyone, but she felt that she owed it to Sheldon. He deserved to understand her better and learn how she'd ended up on the streets. She also owed it to Sarah, to free her at last and grieve for her properly. To let her out of the prison she had put her in. She needed to process the grief, the trauma, and the outright horror of their lives. And to do that, she had to let it out. She had

never let herself feel her pain, or express it, and it was time to stop fighting. Something inside her had broken today, and she could no longer hold back the flood, no longer stop the emotions. The cork had been blown off all that was bottled.

CHAPTER 18

1 9 7 3

Jodi could hear whimpers, groans, and grunts. They were getting louder and louder, and she suddenly realized they were coming from Sarah. She ran over to her and saw that Sarah was sweating profusely, her hair and nightgown both soaked.

"What's wrong, Sarah?" she asked in a terrified voice. "Are you okay? Should I go grab Sister Margaret?"

"No, please don't. I just have a stomach-ache. I need help going to the washroom. I've been trying all night, but I can't go, and my stomach is hurting more and more," Sarah said, out of breath and panting hard.

"Okay, come on. I'll help you," Jodi said, pulling Sarah's arm over her shoulder.

"No wait—" Sarah grunted again, as she leaned back on the bed bearing down with her legs spread, she screamed.

By now, most of the little girls had been woken up. They circled Sarah's bed, their little faces taut with worry.

Sarah began to scream louder and louder, and they could hear Sister Mary storming towards the room. The little girls hurried

back to their beds, but remained upright, their tiny little hands grasped tight against their hearts.

Sister Mary entered the room, snapping on the lights, and stormed over to the bed. She lifted Sarah's nightgown and saw Sarah's vagina bulging, a bulbous little furry thing poking out of it. The little girls screamed.

Sister Mary turned to them, yelling, "Rise to your feet! Rise and bear witness to the penance this succubus shall pay for using her evil in seducing a man of God! Sarah is a wolf in sheep's clothing! She has committed sins beyond forgiveness and will never go to heaven. She will burn at the gates of hell!" Her loud voice pierced their ears.

Sarah let out a deafening scream then, and the door burst open. Father Michael gasped in horror at the scene before him.

"Sister Margaret!" he called back over his shoulder, as she followed him into the room and rushed forward. Looking down at Sarah's swollen vagina, she set to work. "I need blankets, children, and hot water, and as many towels as you can find," she ordered. Three little girls ran off hurriedly to find them. She told three others to come over to the bedside and another one to get a cold wet cloth. "Place it on her forehead and keep her cool."

Sister Margaret looked at Jodi and summoned one of the other little girls. "You two go on either side of her," she said in a surprisingly calm voice. "Pull her knees up as far as you can towards her ears, and don't let go." She turned to Sarah then. "Sssh, sssh, sssh," she whispered gently. "Sarah, I need you to bear down with your tummy and push."

Sarah grunted and screamed, over and over, stopping only to

pant loudly in between pushes to catch her breath.

"Girls, I want you to sing your pretty songs. Sing them loudly to help calm Sarah. She will be okay. I promise. Just sing for her."

The little girls started to sing, their voices trembling and not quite on key, though they tried their best. A large gush of fluid burst from Sarah's vagina then, and out slipped what looked like a little rubbery doll. They all gasped, including Sarah, who was trying to look over her knees to see what it was, the pain in her abdomen suddenly gone.

Sister Margaret put the little doll on her lap and patted its back. After a quick cough, the doll began to cry.

"It's a baby!" squealed one of the little girls. "It's a baby!!"

There was complete silence as Sister Margaret wiped off the baby, who was covered in blood and a white, sticky layer that looked like baking lard. She handed Sarah the baby then, and the young mother held her child in her arms, looking down at it in amazement, a small, contented smile on her face.

"It's a girl, Sarah," Sister Margaret told her.

All the little girls gathered around. "What's her name? What's her name?" they asked excitedly, jumping up and down.

Sister Mary, whom they'd all forgotten about suddenly snapped. "It has no name!" She stormed over and grabbed the baby from Sarah's arms.

Sarah reached for her baby, tears streaming down her face. "Please, Sister Mary! Please! Just let me hold her!"

Father Michael ran and grabbed the baby from Sister Mary. "Stop!" he commanded in a loud angry voice. "Sister, you must leave immediately!"

"B-But, Father," she stammered, her face shocked and confused at the admonishment. "She needs to be punished for her sins against God, and against you!"

"OUT!" he screamed at her with a spray of spittle. "Get out! Now!!"

Completely stunned, Sister Mary froze in place, just looking at Father Michael as though he had gone mad.

He gritted his teeth and set his jaw, preparing for the venom he was about to spit at her. "Woman, let me make myself crystal clear, you will get out of this room, and away from this school, this very moment."

Without another word, Sister Mary turned on her heels and stormed out of the room.

Father Michael handed the baby over to Sister Margaret, who stared at him with knowing eyes until he broke the connection. Father Michael looked at the floor then and put his hand to his forehead, shaking it in exasperation as he walked away.

Sister Margaret followed his exit with her eyes before turning her attention back to Sarah. "Here, darling. Here is your daughter." She gently placed the tiny girl into her mother's arms, then leaned over and kissed Sarah on the forehead.

"Jodi, come with me and get a bottle," she said then. "The rest of you go to the dining room for some toast and tea."

Jodi followed Sister Margaret to the infirmary, watching as she filled a bottle with warm milk. "It's all we have. Go and be with Sarah and have her feed the baby." With that, Sister Margaret turned and walked briskly and purposefully down the hall. Jodi watched after her and saw her enter Father Michael's study.

Jodi returned quietly to the room and watched as Sarah rocked the baby, who was cooing and sucking on Sarah's fingers. Jodi passed her the bottle and watched as she put the nipple in the baby's mouth. The baby closed its eyes and started to suck greedily.

Sarah looked up at her. "They're going to take her, aren't they?" she asked, with tears in her eyes. Heartbroken, Jodi looked at her, not knowing what to say, though they both knew the answer.

"Her name is Memengwaa," Sarah said holding her baby tight and rocking her. Jodi left the room then to give Sarah some time alone with her baby, and as she exited, she heard Sarah humming to her little girl through her tears.

Jodi went back into the infirmary and saw Sister Margaret packing up her belongings.

"Hang in there, darling. You are strong, brave, and beautiful, and your heart is pure. Sarah will need you." She patted Jodi's shoulder on her way out of the room. Jodi watched from the window as Sister Margaret walked outside and got into a waiting car.

In almost the exact moment that Sister Margaret's car pulled out of the gates, a large black limousine pulled up in front of the school. Jodi watched as a well-dressed man, wearing a black hat, crawled out of the driver's side of the car. He walked around to the right side of the vehicle and opened the door for the occupants within. A few moments later, he helped a beautiful white woman, dressed in furs, out of the car. He took her hand gently, guiding her safely out of the vehicle. She was followed by a sharp-looking man in a dark suit. The man laid a hand on her back as they walked up the stairs into the school.

Not long thereafter, she heard Sarah's screams. "No! No, no, no! Please! Please, don't take her! I'll take care of her! I promise! I'll leave and take her with me, and I'll never mention to anyone that I was ever here! PLEASE!"

Jodi ran into the room to see Sarah, reaching for her baby, sobbing, her face swollen with tears. Wailing, her heart visibly shattering, Sarah watched Father Michael take the baby from her and leave the room.

Jodi lay down with her and held her tight, kissing her and stroking her hair. Sarah cried for what felt like forever, until she was finally exhausted, and there were no more tears left to fall.

As Sarah's sobs slowly subsided, turning into soft mournful sounds, she finally fell asleep, gifting her at least a brief recess from her grief.

Jodi left Sarah's bed, tucking her in snugly, and walked back to the empty nursing station. She looked out the window once again and watched as the well-dressed man and the woman descended the outdoor steps. The woman was carrying the small baby bundled in a pink blanket in her arms. She watched as Sarah's little butterfly floated away, taking her mother's heart with her.

The baby would never know her mother, and her mother would never know her. Jodi turned away from the window as the car pulled out and drove off with Sarah's baby. Then she sat on the floor and cried until she heaved and choked.

Sarah didn't leave her bed that night, or the following day. She refused to speak to anyone. She wailed day and night, stopping only to sleep. Her face was blotchy, red, and almost

unrecognizable. Jodi and the little girls took turns holding her, sleeping with her, and brushing her hair. But as much as they tried to console her, they were unable to penetrate her wall of grief. By the third night, the nuns had grown weary of her and called a doctor to perform a bedside assessment.

"She has melancholy," the doctor diagnosed. "After having a baby, they always get sick with it. It will pass. In the meantime, here is a sedative to keep her quiet, and some medication to lift her mood."

Day after day, it continued like this. The nuns would administer the sedative and medicate her, and Sarah would lie in bed, glassy eyed, staring at the ceiling. Sarah's medicine came at precise times, and before she received it, Jodi and the little girls would help her to the bathroom, bathe her, and comb her hair. Sarah was frail, nothing but skin and bones. No matter how much Jodi tried, she could not convince Sarah to eat or drink.

It seemed like weeks had passed. Sarah no longer cried, but she was listless, in a near catatonic state. There was no light left in her eyes. There was absolutely nothing any of them hadn't tried to get Sarah to respond. All they could do was continue to love her and hope that, in time, she would come around.

One of the new nuns came to see Sarah that night.

"That is quite enough of this, Sarah," she barked. "You're quite lucky you were not thrown out on the street for your terrible indiscretion. You will be out of bed tomorrow and resume your studies. There will be no more moping."

Sarah didn't move or speak. She just lay there. The nun huffed, turned on her heels, and walked out of the room.

After the nun had left, Jodi crawled under the covers with Sarah and rubbed her back. Sarah rolled over on her side and faced Jodi.

"I love you," Sarah whispered, her voice barely audible.

"I love you too," Jodi replied, kissing her forehead, wrapping her arms around her, and pulling her in close. Sarah wrapped her own arms around her then, and Jodi breathed a huge sigh of relief. Sarah was coming around, and soon she would be back to normal. Jodi held her closer and stroked her hair. She was going to be there always to help Sarah heal, and one day, they would live together on a farm with dogs and horses just like they had always dreamed. Jodi smiled at this and fell asleep with Sarah in her arms.

Jodi awoke abruptly as a scream shattered the silent night. She jumped out of bed and ran out to the hall where she heard another piercing scream from down below, as well the commotion of the clergy running to see what was wrong. Jodi looked over the banister then and saw Sarah hanging from it by a thick, brown rope. Her neck was at an odd angle, her face was swollen, and her eyes bulged. A puddle of urine was on the floor beneath her. Jodi and the little girls screamed in unison.

Jodi ran down the steps to the main hall, tripping over half of them and falling down on her bottom, catching herself over and over only to fall again. She ran as fast as she could to Sarah but was stopped and held back by the clergy. "NOOOOO!! SARAH! NOOOOO!" she screamed, not stopping as they tried to drag her from the room. "YOU KILLED HER! YOU KILLED HER!! YOU TOOK HER BUTTERFLY AWAY! YOU DID THIS! THIS IS ON YOU!!"

She became combative now, spitting, biting, punching, and kicking them, so wild was she in her grief. The last thing she saw before they held her down and sedated her were Sarah's feet trembling as they dangled, her body still swinging back and forth.

Jodi woke up the next evening with a mouth full of cotton. Two little girls lay on either side of her, snuggling her. For a moment, she took comfort in their closeness. Their warm, innocent, sweaty, little bodies all tangled up in hers. Jodi smelled their hair and skin and listened to their little snores. It all came flooding back to her then. She looked over to Sarah's empty bed, and her heart broke all over again.

She untangled herself from the children and tucked them in nice and snug, giving each of them a kiss on the cheek. Then she opened Sarah's drawer and looked way into the very back. She knew Sarah kept a tiny white piece of paper taped to the top of the drawer there, where it would never be seen. Jodi took it and held it in her hands. There was a small, delicate chain with a butterfly charm folded inside the paper. It was the only thing Sarah had managed to hide when she was taken in, Jodi could never figure out how Sarah had managed it.

Sarah's mother has stuffed it into her hands as she was ripped from her arms. When Sarah and Jodi were alone, they would hold it and pray to it. They prayed that the butterfly would grow really big one night and carry them both back to Sarah's mother. Jodi would watch Sarah at night, swinging the necklace like a pendulum for hours. Then she would hold it to her heart, kiss it, and place it back into its hiding place. Years later, Jodi would pawn that necklace to get her fix.

Sounds and light woke Jodi up, and she went over to the window to see what was happening out there at this hour of the night. There was a floodlight set up in the field adjacent to the schoolyard, just outside the fence. There were two men out there wiping sweat off their foreheads. They leaned on their shovels and shared water between them while they rested, then walked away into the shadows. When they returned, she watched in horror as they swung Sarah's body back and forth a few times before tossing it into the hole. Jodi knew it was Sarah. Who else could it have been? Besides, she had seen the large spot of white on her forearm that bled into the darkness of the surrounding skin. Sarah had the same patches on her face, hands, and tummy. It was a skin condition of some sort, which accentuated her features, making her uniquely beautiful. Sarah hated it and became upset when she noticed the patches were spreading further. But Jodi could only wish she had Sarah's beautiful skin. She'd never seen anything like it before and had never seen anyone more beautiful.

That was enough, Jodi knew she had to get out of there once and for all. Sarah had been the only thing keeping her there. They had made many plans to escape, but Sarah would always get cold feet at the last minute. After this had happened several times, Jodi stopped asking Sarah and resigned herself to whatever life lay before them. Jodi would have never left Sarah no matter how bad it got. But now she was gone.

Jodi went back to her bed and grabbed her clothes, then tiptoed into the nursing station, scanning the hallways to make sure that no one was around. She slowly opened the fridge and grabbed some apples and juice boxes, and a few handfuls of

saltine crackers. Just as she was about to head back, she looked over and saw a chair with a large bag on it. She dumped out the belonging in the purse and put her food and drinks inside. There were a few crumpled bills and a handful of change as well. Jodi looked at them and was tempted to take it. No, she thought, thou shall not steal.

Jodi was still innocent enough to have morals and values. For now.

She tiptoed back into the room and looked at the little girls sleeping in their beds. She was sick to her stomach, knowing that she'd be abandoning these motherless children, but pushed it aside, knowing there was no more that she could do for them. This would be just the first of many emotions that Jodi would repress. That day was the day that Jodi started to grow her outer protective shell. Over time, it would become so hardened that she failed to even notice when her mind and heart left her without saying goodbye.

Jodi walked slowly down the stairs and stopped at the bottom. She brought up short, shivering, and frozen, looking at where Sarah had hung ... where she had taken her very last breath. Jodi didn't think she could move. Her body was slicked with sweat, and she started to hesitate. This was a bad idea. What was she thinking? Who knew what was out there? Here was safe, albeit relatively. It was, at least, predictable, and familiar. Once she passed through that front door though, everything would be foreign. But something was urging her ... pulling her toward the door. Jodi took a deep breath, let go, and surrendered her fate to the universe. With that choice, she took her first step onto the road less travelled.

Jodi ran, and she ran, and she ran. She didn't stop running until her legs cramped and her lungs burnt. Out of steam, she dropped into a crumpled heap on the ground. She was slicked with sweat and gasping for air. Her mouth was so dry that it made it difficult to swallow. As she lay there waiting for her hammering heart to slow, she realized that she was completely alone. She had gotten away with it. No one had chased her down. She was free from hell. The only sounds she could hear were that of nature. The calm, peaceful chirping of birds and the trill of cicadas. Bliss. She stared up at the sunny skies and smiled. She lay there for hours, basking in the heat of the sun, content and excited about the future, until her happiness and good fortune ran out once more.

Jodi watched as the clouds moved in, robbing her of her moment of peace. She heard the boom of thunder, saw the crack of lightning, and then the rain started pouring down. She realized quickly that she had nowhere to go. She became aware that she was uncomfortably hungry and yearned for cold water to satiate her burning throat.

It wasn't long before the regrets started to seep in. She had no shelter, food, or money. She had not formulated a plan as to how she would survive should she be successful in her escape. Panic began to rise, her slowing heart racing again. Jodi closed her eyes and took a deep breath in an attempt to quell her anxiety. In the background, far away, she thought she could just make out

the sound of distant traffic, so she climbed to her feet and headed towards the sound, praying that she would find some help.

Dex had just sorted out his working girls; picking them up, dropping them off, and running interference for a girl whose John had refused to pay. Business had been booming the last few years, but the number of useful girls on his roster had lately started declining. He couldn't keep up with the demand, and his loyal clientele were starting to move on and take their business elsewhere. Some of the girls were pregnant, and most so badly hooked on drugs that they were useless. His younger, prettier girls had lost their youth, their beauty replaced by the makeup of meth: frailty, missing hair, scabs, rotting or missing teeth.... These girls didn't get paid what it cost to feed them, so he slowly released them onto the strip to find their own way. He still had many of these largely worthless women, but young fresh meat was hard to find.

Oddly, a lot of his girls had also disappeared. It was laughable to imagine that they'd gotten clean, moved into houses in the suburbs, and married doctor or lawyers. There was an acceptable, expected amount loss in this business, from overdoses, suicide, and wanderers, thinking that maybe the grass would be greener in the next town. But these were a lot more than the average losses. It seemed like every time he turned around, another one of them was gone. There was talk of a predator on the prowl, and it seemed like his woman were its easiest prey.

All of this contributed to a dwindling bank account, and the sand in his hourglass had nearly run out. Dex needed girls—young ones—and he needed them now. He had scoured the bus stations and the shelters, checked out the hypersexualized bad girls at high school ... anywhere he could think to find new talent. Dex knew them by their look. He could see the vulnerability stained on their faces. The ones that wanted to get away from their uptight parents, the ones who had escaped an abusive home, the heartbroken, the desperate, the unloved, and the unwanted. They were all putty in his hands. Easy pickings. He hadn't been having too much luck as of late though and was beginning to get frustrated. Just as he was going to spin his car around and drive home, Dex saw her ... and smiled.

Dex carefully pulled the car to the side of the road and cranked the heat up, then grabbed a blanket from the backseat. Now was the time to slather on the charm. As he approached her, the girl startled, but there was no mistaking the hidden relief in her eyes.

"Ssshhh," Dex said softly as he placed the blanket around her shivering body. "I bet you could use some warm clothes and a hot meal."

Although not allowing him to see her quiet desperation, Jodi did not need any coaxing to get in the car. Jodi climbed in, immediately placing her hands over the heating vents. Dex watched her body shudder violently as the cold in her body was replaced by heat. He waited for her to get comfortable. When she started to get warm and relaxed a bit, he turned to her and introduced himself.

"My name is Dex," he said pleasantly.

She told him her name was Jodi. Dex took her to a local coffee shop and bought her a hot chocolate and a muffin, which she ate greedily. He could tell that she hadn't eaten for a while. He watched as she burnt her tongue trying to get the hot, sugary drink into her belly.

"Slow down," he said, chuckling. "I'll take you to eat a proper meal soon."

Dex drove her to department store next, where she picked out warm, dry jogging clothes, clean undergarments, and toiletries. He removed the tags from her clothing once she had tried them on and threw her waterlogged clothes in the garbage. Jodi was clean and dry and in better spirits. Dex asked her if she would like to go to the diner down the road for a proper meal. She replied with a loud growling stomach making them both laugh. At the diner he watched as she ravenously stuffed forkful after forkful, devouring her meal in record time.

Overfull and content, she laughed, and they made light conversation. Dex could see that the layers of defensive walls she had around her were starting to come down. He needed to tread lightly so as to not put them back up.

"So, Jodi, I can't help but wonder what your story is. Why would a pretty girl like you be sitting in the rain on the side of the road?"

Jodi blushed at the compliment but bristled at the questions. Until now, she had forgotten the past. The question had caught her off guard and slapped her back to reality. She didn't want to share her story. She didn't even want to hear her story.

Dex looked at Jodi, waiting patiently for her response. She took

the time to look at him, to really look at him. His eyes were tender. He spoke to her softly and kindly. He had a French accent that soothed her and made him sound sophisticated and intelligent. He was young and objectively handsome, his face open and warm. His features and demeanour exuded genuine care for her.

Jodi decided to tell him the fringes of her story, just enough for him to get the picture but not enough for him to know the entirety of her life.

Jodi explained to him that she had nowhere to go, but she absolutely could never, ever go back to where she had been. She watched as Dex took a sip of wine and sat back in his chair. He looked up to the right then, with a pondering expression on his face. The silence between them started to become uncomfortable and awkward.

"You know," he said finally, "I am inclined to help you. You look like you've been through quite an ordeal, and the downtown city streets are not safe for a young girl like you. I myself had a little girl once, about your age. Her name was Joyce. Unfortunately, she suffered a fatal accident, and she is no longer with me." He released a sigh that was heavy with sadness. "I miss her dearly."

Jodi's heart broke at the telling of his tale. She had so much sadness and empathy for him as she watched his face fall and a large tear roll down his cheek.

"I think maybe it could be good for the both of us if you came to stay with me. We could have our own little family of sorts. You'll get all the delicious food you could ever want, a nice bedroom, and I have a few simple jobs you could do to earn you some money for school." Jodi looked at him with wide, disbelieving eyes.

"Come on, Jodi," he said then. "You're going to love it. Me and you against the world. A real team. We'll support each other to make things better."

He watched as everything he'd offered her played over and over in her mind. Her face brightened with excitement. "Yes! That sounds ... amazing!"

Once they'd finished eating, and he'd paid their tab, he held her hand and guided her back to the car, holding its door open for her. "You won't regret this," he said triumphantly as they drove back to the city.

Jodi would hear those words in her nightmares for years. It wasn't too long before she realized how terribly wrong, she had been to trust Dex. In hindsight, life with him made the school she'd escaped from feel like heaven. While in Dex's "care," she had learned fast to be weary and mistrustful of others. Regular rough handling had no effect on her. She would not perform her duties unless subjected to extreme violence. Finally, to force her into compliance, she was injected with liquid gold against her will. For a time, as long as the supply was steady, she would allow the most heinous and vile acts to be perpetrated against her.

It wasn't long before she was begging to do absolutely anything for the dope. Blazed out of her mind, she couldn't feel anything; she couldn't remember anything. She could lay in a room for hours while one businessman after another had their way with her.

Of course, with such aggressive handling, her fresh, youthful appeal didn't last long, and she was soon relegated to Dex's "useless" category; dumped onto the strip, where old hookers go to die. Sex, drugs, repeat. During a particularly long dry spell

between clients, with nothing but the clothes on her back and an addiction to heroin, the only source of money she had to her name was Sarah's butterfly necklace. She didn't think twice about pawning it. She needed to score.

CHAPTER 19

1 9 9 1

Sheldon was stunned and sat frozen in shock. He couldn't formulate a response. *How could he respond to something like that?* His stomach hurt. He felt like throwing up. *Why on Earth would anyone do such things to anyone, let alone to little girls? For what purpose?* He looked at Jodi, and couldn't help but imagine her as a child, going through everything she'd just described. His heart was broken.

And what happened to all of those other little girls?

Once Jodi had started, the story had taken on a life of its own. It had exploded out of her in a frenzy, as though it had been lying in wait, ready to pounce the minute the vault was finally opened. Sheldon had listened as Jodi told each terrible detail of her life.

Jodi was exhausted when it was finally over, but Sheldon could tell that a weight had been lifted from her shoulders.

"Jodi, I am so sorry, but thank you so much for trusting me with your pain. We'll help each other heal. Together. I'll be here for you forever. I promise." His eyes were full of

compassion and love. "You need to rest," he said then, guiding her back down to her room and tucking her snugly into bed. "I'm going to go out for a little while, but I'll be back soon, and I'll make us a really nice supper. Would you like that?"

Jodi nodded sleepily. "Before you go, could you please...?" She finished her request with her eyes alone, but Sheldon understood. Nodding, he left the room, returning a few moments later with the little black pouch. Jodi looked at him gratefully.

"You've had one hell of a day, Jodi. Now, close your eyes and have a nap," he said as he gave her a small dose of dope. Sheldon hoped she would sleep just long enough for him to finish his shopping and make supper.

Jodi awoke well rested and took a few minutes to stretch and ready herself to crawl out of bed. When she was ready, she climbed out of bed and stopped dead in her tracks. A small circular table, draped in a red tablecloth, had been set up, with a candle burning at its centre.

Sheldon walked towards her, taking her hand, and guiding her to her place at the table. Jodi looked at him, her eyes brimming with tears of happiness. Sheldon was holding a bouquet of roses.

"I hope you like them," he said, smiling at her shyly. Jodi took them from him and held them to her heart, burying her nose into the plump buds and breathing in their aromatic scent. The roses were beaded in dew and accentuated with baby's breath. Jodi had never seen something so beautiful.

"Sheldon, I have no words. I just.... I'm...." Her voice

trailed off, overwhelmed with emotions that she had no idea how express.

Sheldon came over to her and held her, softly kissing her cheek. "Jodi, I need you to come with me. We need to go for a drive."

"Where?" she asked, confused.

"There is something I need you to see. I believe it's necessary to help you heal."

She smiled at him, but it was strained. This was the absolute last thing she wanted to do in that moment, and her face told him that.

"Please, Jodi," he said, his voice as gentle as she had ever heard it. "For Sarah?"

Jodi relented then and held his hand tight as he blew out the candle. Then he led her upstairs, outside, and into the car. Together, they drove out of the woods and continued on for quite a while before the sights started to become familiar.

"Sheldon, no. Absolutely not. Please turn around," she said, struggling to get her seatbelt off, as though ready to throw herself from the moving vehicle.

He placed his hand on her arm, gently stilling her. "It's okay, Jodi. We need to do this. It'll be alright."

The school stood dark and abandoned now but terrifying, nonetheless. The place of her nightmares.

"Sheldon," she said as she started to cry. "I feel sick. Why did you bring me here?"

Sheldon took her hand and squeezed it tightly as she began to shiver with terror. Pulling up to the school, he parked

and turned off the engine. "I know, Jodi. I know. But I think this is something you have to do. I promise that you *will* feel better once it's finished." Sheldon got out and went around to her side of the car, opening the door and gently pulling her to her feet before placing his arms around her. Holding her close, he started walking them towards the schoolyard.

When they reached the rear fence, the spinning and dizziness started again. Jodi's knees grew weak, and Sheldon caught her before she fell to the ground, scooping her up and carrying her the rest of the way. Jodi's face was buried in his chest, her eyes closed tight.

Sheldon soon arrived, and placed her feet on the ground, making sure that she was steady on her feet. He led her forward. Jodi stopped suddenly and pressed hard against his side as she saw a heart-shaped wreath—with a ribbon bearing Sarah's name across the centre—covered in flowers and paper butterflies.

Jodi fell to her knees, the wind knocked out of her.

Sheldon knelt down behind Jodi, wrapping his arm around her. "Jodi, you never had the chance to say goodbye to her. I wanted you to be able to have somewhere that you could visit her and remember, a place where you could put her to rest."

Jodi saw that there was a heart-shaped rock on the ground where Sarah lay and wanted to reach out to it but found herself unable to move, overwhelmed by grief, gratitude, and love.

Tears poured down her cheeks as the dam busted open, the pressure of her liquid pain exploding forth, carrying with it

all the buried hurt, sadness, and grief.... She allowed herself permission to feel it—to feel it all—as she fell back against Sheldon's chest.

He held her until the stars came out above them.

Finally, she managed to choke out her gratitude in a voice heavy with emotion. "It's perfect, Sheldon. I-I c-can't thank you enough."

"Are you ready?" He asked her, producing two beautiful red roses from inside his jacket.

"Yes," she said. "I am."

Jodi and Sheldon each took a rose. Jodi kissed hers and looked into the heavens where thousands of stars greeted her. They laid their roses and their hands on top of the grave then, each saying the prayers that were important to them, then held each other until the tears stopped. Jodi was finally ready to fully remember Sarah and let her rest in peace.

A long time later, once she had gathered her composure, they returned home and went back downstairs. Sheldon led her to the table, then left her for a quick moment while he ran back upstairs. Jodi sat at the table, her heart full of sorrow, full of love, and full of emotions that she had long suppressed. She had held all of that in for so long that she'd thought it was forgotten, but the body never forgets. To release all that had made her feel lighter, and allowed her to grieve for her mother, her childhood, and for Sarah.

She finally understood herself and all the hurt she'd been trying to bury beneath the drugs. She had suppressed her emotions to the point where the drugs were the only thing

that worked to relieve her pain. She had degraded her body and self-worth to forget. Tonight, though, had been cathartic. Jodi was finally able to find peace, knowing that Sarah was safe and loved and would be with her always.

Jodi heard Sheldon on the stairs, and her mouth watered at the aroma of the meals he was carrying. Jodi realized that she was starving as they sat down to eat the delicious steaks, he had prepared for them. It melted in her mouth, and she couldn't resist a groan.

"Is it good?" he asked her.

"I've never eaten steak, I only imagined what it tasted like!" She laughed as the juices ran down her face. She grabbed her napkin to dry her chin. "I never imagined it would be as good as this. Now I know why people love it so much!"

When they were done, Sheldon gathered their plates and went upstairs, while Jodi stayed seated, admiring the roses he had given her. Sheldon returned with two small, beautiful, delicious-looking cakes. They sat down together and ate in a contented silence. At one point, Jodi put out her hand. Sheldon covered her hand with his and looked at her. There was no need for words. Their eyes told the story of their pain, sorrow, joy, and the appreciation and gratitude they had for one another.

Sometime later, he said softly, "Jodi, could I ask you something?" She looked up at him, nodding that he could. "I've never danced with someone, and it has always been something I wanted to do. Would you dance with me?" He looked a bit embarrassed, unable to meet her eyes.

"I've never actually danced with anyone either," she said with a laugh, "but let's give it a try." They both stood up from the table, and Jodi put her hand in his. Awkwardly, they came together, his hands at her waist, and her arms around the back of his neck.

There was no music, but slowly they moved closer until their chests pressed close together, their hearts beating as one. They both longed for love, touch, warmth, and connection.... These feeling were foreign to both of them, but neither one wanted them to stop. The intensity and tension between them grew. Both of them wanting to react but nervous of the other's reaction. Finally, her heart racing, Jodi looked up at him, placing her hands on either side of his face and pulling him down towards her. Sheldon kissed her forehead and her cheeks. Then he pulled her in, his hand on the back of her head, stroking her hair. Jodi could feel his heart hammering in his chest and the electricity between them; her tummy was full of butterflies. Jodi had never felt this way about a man in her life, and her body had never responded with want, longing, or pleasure. She was finally able to let go because she felt safe and didn't need to worry about being beaten or misused. She could finally let her guard down and release the rigidity in her body.

Sheldon let her free from the embrace and was about to do the gentlemanly thing and walk away, not wanting to make her feel uncomfortable, when Jodi grabbed his hand and pulled him close again, pressing her lips to his. The feeling coursing through their bodies was unexplainable, each

wanting more as passion grew inside them. Neither one of them wanted it to stop.

With cheeks aflame, she was barely able to pull back, out of breath with the lust inside her. In all of her sexual experiences, she had never felt anything at all. She would just stare at whatever was in front of her eyes and wait for it to be over. She had often wondered how in the world people even enjoyed sex, but as she looked at him, she understood.

Jodi pulled him into the bedroom. As they got closer to the canopy bed, she turned from him to release the curtains from their ties, cocooning the bed in safety and comfort.

"I-I ... um... I've n-never—"

"It's okay," she said. "Come here." She pulled him towards the bed, and he lay down beside her. They kissed long and passionately and each moment that passed between them grew deeper and deeper. They were lost in each other; there was no time or space, only them. Out of breath, they stopped, feeling almost completely out of control. Jodi's body was on fire. She sat up and lifted Sheldon's shirt. He tensed up and resisted at first, trying to leave his shirt on. He had never bared his scars to anyone.

"It's ok," she said to him softly and removed her shirt, revealing the same deep scars criss-crossing all over her back. "I'm here," she said reassuringly. "You're safe. I just want to feel your skin on mine." Sheldon pulled her close again, kissing her shoulders and neck with trepidation, still very shy and nervous.

Sheldon pulled back from her and asked her to wait for

a moment. She felt coolness on her body as the air blew between them. She heard him rustling, and then he asked her to sit up. He moved behind her then, placing her hair gently over to the side, baring her neck. Jodi watched as his arms moved around in front of her, his hands resting lightly on either side of her neck. Then she felt a strange coldness, the faint weight of a charm on her chest, and the tickle of a delicate necklace across her collar bones. She looked down, capturing the charm in her hand, and saw that it was a tiny butterfly. It was Sarah's necklace. She gasped. Tears running down her cheeks, she turned to him. "Sheldon, where did you find this?"

"It was right there, still at the pawn shop on the strip after all this time. Sarah must have wanted you to have it," he said to her lovingly. Once again, the tears fell, and he held her tight. She held the little butterfly and turned, looking Sheldon in the eyes. Then he pulled her close, the passion between them igniting again, even hotter, and brighter than before. Sheldon broke away from her one last time, whispering, "I love you."

He looked at her as no one ever had and said words she had not heard since her mother had passed away. He placed his hand on her heart, and she placed her hand on his. They stared into each other's eyes, and then gave their bodies fully to each other. Over and over, they loved each other, each time better than the last. There was nothing but exploration, gentleness, and love. No pain, no hurt, no degradation, just kind and genuine love.

Finally, covered in sweat, their bodies thrumming and exhausted, they cuddled into each other.

"Jodi, do you want your medicine before bed?"

She thought about it, the familiar hunger and growl purring in her chest, but this time was different. This time, she was full. This time, there was no hole to fill. This time, she was already riding a wave of bliss—one that dope had never given her. The feeling she had always been chasing was right there, and it was better than the dope.

"No," she said. "I think I'm done with that." They both fell asleep quickly, holding each other tight all night long.

The next morning, they turned towards each other, kissing, and holding each other tight.

"Sheldon," she said quietly, "I have never made love to anyone before, and I have never felt this kind of happiness for as long as I can remember. I want us to be like this always. I love you."

He pulled her in close and whispered, "I love you too."

The hours passed by as they spent the morning loving each other. When they could finally take no more, they lay with each other, holding on to the afterglow until Jodi's rumbling tummy interrupted.

"We haven't eaten," he said, chuckling. "Come on, let's get cleaned up and go out for breakfast, maybe try again for that shopping trip and walk."

"Okay, okay, okay. I don't want to leave this bed, but we'll need to conserve energy for this evening, I guess." She laughed as she walked towards bathroom. She stopped and turned

to look at him before she went in. "Would you care to join me?" she asked, giving him a look, he couldn't argue with. It didn't take him long to get out of bed.

Sheldon drew her a bath, and she enveloped herself in the loving embrace of the hot, bubbling water. She leaned back and slipped her head under water, wetting her hair and enjoying the heat and the silence. She came back to the surface when she needed a breath, then used her hands to arrange the bubbles so that they were covering her body alluringly.

He smiled at her, clearly enjoying the view. "I want nothing more than to hop right in there," he said, "but first, I would love to wash your beautiful hair."

"Yes, please," she sighed.

Sheldon pulled a stool up behind her, and she could feel him squeeze some shampoo onto the crown of her head. He began to gently massage and lather her hair. The shampoo smelled of almonds, and she inhaled the scent deeply, letting it fill her lungs. Sheldon began to massage her neck and shoulders, going slowly, taking his time. Jodi gave herself over to the feeling of comfort and warmth as she drifted her into a meditative state.

CHAPTER 20

1972

Jodi had heard her name being called, and then repeated, over and over, each time getting louder and louder, and angrier. But she refused to answer. It wasn't her real name.

Sister Mary stood over her desk. "What is your name?" she demanded. Her face was red, and the vein in her forehead looked as if it were about to burst. She stormed over to Jodi's desk at the front of the classroom and withdrew her strap from her belt. "I am going to ask you one more time what your name is!" She spat through clenched teeth.

Jodi could barely understand what Sister Mary was asking her. She had only just begun to learn English. Sister Mary grabbed her and pulled her out of her seat, then bent Jodi over and whipped her. Jodi screamed each time the strap hit her.

"Your name is Jo-di," said Sister Mary, stretching the syllables out.

Struggling not to cry, she answered, "Jodi," in a scared whisper

"What was that? I didn't hear you," Sister Mary said in a condescending tone.

"Jodi. My name is Jodi," she said in a small, defeated voice.

"Yes. Your name is Jodi. You will never refer to yourself again as that mouthful of nonsensical letters. Do you hear me? If you think today's strapping was bad, you will regret what happens to you if I ever hear that name come out of your mouth again."

Sister Mary then wrote "MY NAME IS JODI" in large letters on the chalkboard. "You will write this one hundred times, do you hear me?" she asked. Jodi nodded while she watched the nun stomp out of the classroom. She started to write the lines by copying each letter the nun had written. She had no idea how many times "a hundred" was.

1991

The candle softly illuminated Jodi's face in its flickering glow. She was completely immersed in the bath he had lovingly drawn for her. She looked relaxed, and Sheldon's heart filled with love as he listened to her gentle breaths. He washed her beautiful hair slowly, taking his time, watching as the bubbles ebbed and flowed, revealing a small hint of her cleavage, glistening in the bubbles. Sheldon was totally content to spend this quiet, loving time with her, the likes of which he had only dreamed of. He carefully rinsed her hair, and sat back on his stool, taking in her peacefulness, when all of a sudden, Jodi flailed in the bath, choking and sputtering on the water she had just inhaled. She sat up straight and looked him dead in the eye, "Bineshiin!" she yelled, climbing suddenly from the water. "My name is Bineshiin!"

Jodi squeezed him tight, then pulled back and looked at him with sparkling eyes, full of joy.

"I remember now," she said. "My name is Bineshiin." She said this proudly and kept repeating the name over and over as if in disbelief.

He grinned at her. "I told you that you didn't look like a Jodi." Then more seriously, he took her chin and tipped it up. "Hello, Bineshiin. It is so nice to meet you." With that, he kissed her lips, and she started jumping up and down in his arms, laughing. She had finally grown her wings.

Sheldon and Bineshiin got ready and left the house, and she did so with her head held high. There was no past; there was no future. There was only today, and today, her head felt clear, her heart felt love, and she was full to the brim with happiness and gratitude.

Sheldon held open the door for her. "Madam," he said, laughing.

"Why, thank you, Sir." She giggled. She kissed him passionately then before getting into the passenger seat. She looked around the car and was jolted with a quick flash of familiarity. She had pulled a thousand tricks in a thousand cars, most of them while she was high, so it wasn't surprising that she'd been in a car similar to this at one time or another. "Sheldon, when you found me, did you pick me up in this car?"

"Yes, I did. It's the only one we have. I am not supposed to use it actually, but Father's in jail, so I guess it is all ours!" He laughed.

Fuzzy flashes of memory danced around at the back of her mind. She dismissed it though, chalking it up to an unconscious snippet from her initial ride home with Sheldon.

She loved the beauty of the woods, with the sun shining through the branches overhead. "It's beautiful here."

"Hmm.... Yeah, you're right. I guess I never really thought much about it, but yes, when you stop and look at it—truly look at it, I mean—it is quite beautiful."

"Sheldon? I cannot shake the feeling that this is something ... I don't know. Something *more*. That this is destiny," she

said, looking at him seriously.

"Yes, Bineshiin, I do."

It filled her heart to hear her real name on his lips. It was fluid, organic, as though he had always known her this way.

"I knew it the moment I found you," Sheldon said. He recounted to her the events of that evening that had led him to her.

"Sheldon, before my mother died, she told me that, even though I would suffer, I was to never deviate from my journey, and that everything would come around full circle. Not only did you save me from certain death, but you brought me back to my memories of Sarah, and of my mother. You have completed my circle," she told him.

"And you have completed mine, Bineshiin. We've suffered for this love, for this life, but finally, we've both found what we've always wanted and deserved ... in each other." Sheldon took her hand in his.

Soon, they arrived at the methadone clinic in town, where Bineshiin was given a prescription that would help her avoid withdrawal symptoms. After that, they went to the mall and milled about, window shopping, and drinking coffee. Bineshiin looked at their reflection in the store windows. Just another couple, doing what normal couples do. She felt bliss just being there and walking with him. They tried on funny clothes, and they bought some nice things for themselves. They just talked and walked and laughed.

In her past life, she would only go to the mall to try to warm up, and only if it were absolutely unavoidable. People would

stare at her and sharply veer away as if she were contagious. Bineshiin had been removed from the mall so many times that she would rather freeze outside than meet those disgusted stares. Yet, here she was, and no one was giving her more than a cursory glance. She had been accepted into the same society that had shunned her only a few weeks earlier. It sickened her. She felt such resentment and anger.

She also couldn't help but feel like a traitor to the streets, to those who hadn't found an escape and to those who never would. She felt a call to action. She needed to do something to help her brothers and sisters. She would never be able to close the gap in society, but maybe she could help to make it smaller.

"Sheldon, in a few days, when we're feeling more settled, I want to take you to see an old friend. I have some ideas about the school." If she was going to be a part of this society, she was going to do everything in her power to help as many people as she could.

She smiled just thinking about it. "I think there's a way to reframe our hurt into something beautiful, and my friend is the perfect person to help us do it."

"I'm all ears, Bineshiin."

"Let me think on it for a bit. I have a plan," she said, feeling more optimistic, "I just need to develop it."

They enjoyed a nice lunch together, and then went to the grocer to buy some treats for the evening, and ingredients for supper.

"We need to get enough so we can hunker down a few days.

I do not intend on leaving our room," Sheldon said.

"Me neither," she said, both of them laughing.

They pulled into the driveway, and Sheldon grabbed most of the bags. Bineshiin turned to grab the last few from the back seat, but as she picked them up, she screamed, dropping all of the groceries on the ground.

Sheldon ran to her. "Bineshiin, my god! What's wrong?"

Bineshiin was paralyzed, her body rock hard and unmoving. Sheldon looked into the back seat and noticed a pink shoe and a red lollipop stuck to the floor. Confused, he looked back at her. There was a mask of pure terror on her face, and she was blubbering nonsensical words. She put her hands to her throat as though she were choking. Her face was red, and she was wheezing as she gasped for breath.

She was still hyperventilating and would pass out soon if she didn't calm her breathing. Her hands were tearing at her throat, and her eyes were bulging. Sheldon had never been so scared. Bineshiin seemed beyond terror. He ran to the bathroom and grabbed a bath towel, soaking it in freezing water before running back to her. He placed the towel across the back of her neck, and then he sat with her, coaching her to breathe. "Breathe in for four seconds, hold it for four seconds, and breathe out for four seconds...." They did this over and over again. Slowly, Bineshiin's heart rate and breathing calmed. Finally, she removed the towel and looked at him, her skin chalk white. "It was your father." Her voice trembled.

Sheldon looked at her, confused. "In the car?" He gave her

time to find her words, keeping quiet as Bineshiin slowly told him everything. She told him about Katie's death, about seeing the shoe and lollipop in the John's car, and about the brutal rape that she was lucky to have survived. "It's him Sheldon. He did this to Katie, and he did this to me."

Sheldon began to comprehend all that she had told him, all the little puzzle pieces locking into place. Sheldon was no stranger to Father's brutal violence, and no stranger to the combined look of malice and pleasure in his eyes. He looked at Bineshiin, and his heart almost stopped beating as he was struck by a sudden realization. "Oh, my fucking god!" Horror washed over him.

"The room!" they said in unison, both of them bolting towards the basement stairs.

Sheldon and Bineshiin busted into the room and turned it upside down. The room was there for some evil reason, and they needed to know what it was. Bineshiin dumped the hampers of wool and plush animals on the bed and started to sort through them, while Sheldon ripped apart drawers.

She noticed a small, white paddle painted with hearts and bears, hanging from the wall with ribbons. She walked over to it and picked it up. Sheldon came up behind her, and as she turned it around, they both saw a name stenciled there with pink paint: Lucy.

Bineshiin dropped the paddle on the ground.

"Lucy was real, and this was her room!" Bineshiin said to Sheldon incredulously.

They pulled out drawers, cleared shelves, and looked under

the bed, but found nothing. Sheldon stopped suddenly. When he was a boy, he'd hidden his most treasured things in his closet to keep them away from Father. Had Lucy done the same?

He rushed over to the closet and started pushing through a little pile of belongings in the back. He gasped as he found a plump little baby doll. The baby had little pink booties, and a little pink dress with a hood trimmed in soft white fur. Underneath the doll, he found a pink journal, covered in dust, and yellowed with age. Sheldon opened the journal and inside the front jacket, he saw the name Lucy, painstakingly penned in swirly writing, and decorated with little flowers. He and Bineshiin fell to the floor, opening the journal, and disappearing into Lucy's life. They read the first few entries, which were poems and stories, describing outings she had gone on with her mom and dad, and adventures with her friends. But soon the horror began.

CHAPTER 21

Saturday!!!!!!!!!!!!!!!!!!!!!!!!!!!!!!
I went to the playground today. That sad man was there again.
I gave him a piece of gum!!!! That made him happy. I am going
to draw him a picture tomorrow.

Sunday
That old man didn't come today. I'll have to bring him a picture
another day. Jillian threw sand at Robbie and got it in his eyes.
He was mad and went home. Probably going to tell his mommy.
He is such a baby.

Monday
I hate Monday. Whoever made Monday should be put in a
rocket and flown to the moon. I did win in a race against Becca
though! Whoever won got to be Andrea's friend, and I won!!
Too bad so sad, Becca!

Wednesday

Sorry for not writing last night, it was my b-day! I am 8. I celebrated my birthday at the hospital. I had gymnastics, and I fell down and hurt my wrist, and we had to go to the hospital. It was just a sprain, but I got a milkshake on the way home!!!

Thursday

Guess what! The sad man came back. He said he was sad because his dog had gone to heaven. I showed him my gymnastic moves, and he laughed and said he wasn't sad anymore. He showed me a science experiment! He put some Mentos in some Pepsi, and it exploded! Best part ever? He gave me the leftover Mentos. I gave him the picture I coloured too, and he said it was the best picture he'd ever seen! Can you believe it?! He said he would be coming back on Friday, and he would have a massive surprise for me!!!

Saturday

Haven't written in a few days. I'm having too much fun! Sad man, his name is Frank by the way, good thing he told me, I think it be weird if I kept calling him the sad man hahaha! He took me to get ice cream and candies yesterday and said I could buy whatever I wanted. Guess what the surprise was???? A kitten! He said I could keep her! I love her so much!! I named her Giorgia! He even said he called Daddy and that I could keep her, and that I could stay with Frank for a big sleepover!!!!!

His house was in the woods, and it looked kind of scary. He

said not to judge a book by its cover, and he was right! I got my own room!!

It's so cute, all pink and white with a huge bed, and I even got my own bathroom! I forgot my clothes....ugh...Frank (ill never get that right) got me a whole bunch more. The coolest part is that my room is in plastic!!!! He said he wanted to make it like a little dollhouse. It's so funny too because there is a doll house in the "doll house."

Sunday

I'm so excited today!!! Mommy and Daddy had to go away for a little while and said I could stay with Frank for the whole time they are gone!! I wished so much that I could stay longer and now I get to! Frank said I didn't even need to go to school anymore!!! No more teachers, no more books, no more Becca's dirty looks hahahahaha. Oh my God! I forgot! This is the bestest news ever! I cannot believe I waited this long to tell you!! Frank gave me a beautiful little baby doll!!! She has a pink dress with a little cloak, like Red Riding Hood, except the hood's got white fur on it. I absolutely love it!! Frank got me wool too so I can knit. Giorgia loves the wool! We spent all morning playing with it. Mommy taught me to knit. I miss her.
☹☹☹☹☹

Frank told me but I forgot

I don't know what day it is really. Frank gives me vitamins every

night, and they make me sleepy. Last night I dreamed that I woke up in middle of the night and he was watching me while I was sleeping. It was weird because my nightgown was on the floor. My private parts are really sore, and it hurts to pee. I can barely walk. Frank said I'm probably allergic to the soap, and he gives me medicine to make me feel better. It doesn't hurt anymore after the medicine, but it feels like I'm asleep for days.

?????

Frank said its my birthday today. Every other day seems like its my birthday. I think I had 4 birthdays, or maybe 5.

Halloween?

I can't remember much anymore. I think its Halloween because the doorbell rang all night. Probably not though, probably another dream. There's something wrong with me. I'm sure. I am sick all the time and I can't eat much. My tummy is really round and swollen. Frank says it's normal and that once I stop taking the vitamins it will go away. Frank keeps standing outside the glass naked. It makes my tummy sick. At first, I thought I was dreaming but now I know I'm not. I try to pretend I'm asleep

Still not sure

Frank hurt Giorgia today. She scratched him, and he really hurt her. She hasn't moved in a long time. My belly hurts. I'm so sad.

I miss my mommy and daddy. Frank isn't nice to me anymore. He really hurts me.

Friday......maybe

It's been a long time since Mommy and Daddy left. They didn't come on any Christmases. I was really sad this year. Frank said they had tried to get home but there was a snowstorm. They haven't even been able to call because there are no phones where they are. Frank said they'll call someday soon.

Giorgia ran away. Frank said cats do that. Frank said if I'd taken better care of the cat she would have stayed. I didn't eat my supper tonight because I was so sad about Georgia. Frank held me down and jammed forkfuls of food in my mouth until I threw up. He was so mad he took off his belt. I don't remember anything. I am in a lot of pain. I cannot move. My night gown is full of blood, and I can't take it off. It's too sticky and if I try to it hurts even more.

I don't know anymore

It is way after Christmas, I think this is the 3rd, 4th, or even the 5th Christmas or maybe it is the same one. I don't know anything anymore. Frank said Mommy and Daddy decided they don't love me anymore. They had a new baby and moved away. I couldn't stop crying all day. Today he burned my arms with scalding water in the bath because I wouldn't stop crying. Now I can't stop crying because my arms are burnt. Frank keeps hurting me.

He keeps hitting me over and over with a paddle. Sometimes he hits me so much that I can't get up out of bed.

I know that there is a baby in my tummy. Frank said all girls get babies in their belly and there was nothing to be afraid of. I remember Mommy's friend had a belly like this, and it turned into a baby. Frank said it would be just like my doll. I knit the baby a blanket. Mommy gave her friend a baby blanket. I finished it. It's yellow. Frank asked me what I would name it if it was a girl. I said Giorgia. Frank said if it's a boy, his name will be Sheldon. I'm tired now. My tummy has been hurting for two days. I don't know how I got a baby in my belly, and I don't know how it's going to come out.

CHAPTER 22

Bineshiin and Sheldon looked at each other silently for a long time.

"Sheldon," he said. "I am Sheldon. Lucy was his mother..." They sat in stunned silence. Day turned to night, with neither of them speaking, both lost in deep reflection. There would be moments where the shock would hit them fresh again, the reality sickening them as it rippled through their bodies.

"We need to go. We need to get help, Sheldon," she said. He looked up at her in shock and dismay. "Sheldon, we need to go to the police. Come on. I'll go with you." He still sat there frozen, his eyes blank and unseeing. "Sheldon!" she yelled, shaking him. "We have to go now!"

He finally snapped out of his daze and got up. They started up the stairs, but Bineshiin paused, touching his back. "Wait." Sheldon turned around to look at her. "I need to grab her journal."

She ran quickly back to the room to get it, and then heard a loud thump. She turned back to see Sheldon falling backwards down the stairs. "Sheldon!" she screamed. She dropped the journal and ran towards him. His face was covered in

blood, his eyes rolled back in his head, and he wasn't moving.

She was standing there in complete shock when she heard heavy footsteps slowly descend the stairs. Then, there was Frank, looking at her with black eyes full of savagery, with no thread of humanity left in them.

"Well, hello there! I think we have met before!" Frank smiled.

She took a step back without even realizing she had moved.

"No? Well, either way, I am so glad you are here. It's been a long time since I had a girl down here. You're older than I'd like, and definitely not much to look at, but you'll do. You can stay as long as you like. Wouldn't that be nice?" His eyes sparkled with malice as they bore into hers.

Bineshiin watched as he licked his lips and set his jaw. She saw the primal hunger in him; he was ready to pounce at her slightest movement. He wanted to hunt for his food and play with it; it was clear he had no desire for a quick meal. They never broke eye contact. She knew that this time, she wouldn't be getting away from him alive. Her knees felt weak, and she couldn't swallow. All the saliva in her mouth had completely dried up. Her heart palpated as it raced, *would she be so lucky to die on the spot? No, she wouldn't, luck was rarely ever on her side.*

She was paralyzed, knowing he'd be on her if she so much as blinked. The anxiety of waiting for it made her feel like she could no longer breathe. She was facing her death, staring it straight in the eyes, and she knew that it would be brutal and savage. She still remembered his teeth tearing her skin.

Warm urine ran down her leg then, making a puddle on the floor beneath her. This was exactly what he wanted. Fear. He wanted power. Control. He wanted to inflict pain slowly, drawing it out. Frank wanted to be God.

Frank came forward then leaning in until his face was an inch from hers. Their noses were almost touching, and she could smell his sweat and the rankness of his breath. "BOO!!" he screamed in her face, and she turned and ran. He just stood there, smiling, and watching her. She was a mouse stuck in a trap. She'd never get past him. She had nowhere to go. Eventually, as he maxed out on the pleasure of watching her cower, he walked purposefully towards her, watching her face contort in terror with each step. He had weeks to drag this out ... as long as he could rein in his need and avoid being hasty.

Frank could barely believe it, but his son had finally done something right. A chip off the old block. He was proud to see that Sheldon had brought one home on his own and served her up to him on a silver platter. Frank had already been excited to come home and knock the sight out of Sheldon's eyes for leaving him in jail so long, but now his refusal to come get him made sense. Sheldon had been readying this surprise for him and had likely wanted to have some uninterrupted time to take his share of the prize before having to share. He actually felt badly for hitting the kid now.

Bineshiin knew she had nowhere to go; she looked over to see Sheldon still crumpled on the ground, near death or dead. There was a pool of blood coming from his head. She

had no options left. She cowered in the corner, watching as Frank removed his clothes.

He was enjoying this. Every minute of it. Frank watched as she scanned the room, looking for something, anything, with which to defend herself. Bineshiin grabbed Lucy's paddle from the wall, and Frank groaned in pleasure, just looking at it. That would be the perfect implement to start with. He'd rip it easily from her hands.

Bineshiin backed herself further and further into the corner. All she had was the paddle, and she definitely didn't think it would be of much help. She had to try though. She'd made it this far in life, and if she was going to die, she'd die fighting. She watched as he walked towards her, naked and aroused, staring at her as if he were a wild animal. She watched as spit ran down his chin, his body wired with excitement.

They stood very still, just staring at each other, each waiting for the other to make the first move. Bineshiin decided to strike first, thinking that maybe she could incapacitate him just long enough to pass him and out the door. It was her one and only chance. She ran toward him, using all her force to crack him in the head with the paddle. Frank easily overcame her before she even came close.

Frank was smiling at her with a mouth full of yellowing teeth. Her only defense was to tuck herself into a ball as tight as she could, protecting her head and face with her arms. She cowered there for what felt like forever, staring at his feet. She knew he was feeding off her fear, lording his power over her and breathing it all in. Her terror increased more and

more, waiting for the violence to start.

Frank knelt down in front of her. "Put your arms down," he said gently.

Her body was frozen. She couldn't move her limbs if she tried.

"Put your arms down," he said again, this time more force-fully.

Bineshiin was paralyzed.

"You wouldn't want me to hurt you...." he said manically.

Frank reached his arm around the back of her neck and grabbed her braid, pulling it down so that her face turned up to his. Bineshiin looked deep into his eyes, waiting for what she knew was coming. He bent down and put his mouth on hers; disgust pooled in the back of her throat and revulsion rippled through her. He tasted like cigarettes and booze, and she had to swallow her own bile.

She toyed with the idea of biting down on his tongue as hard as she could, and honestly, she should have just done it. Even if she didn't survive, she'd at least have taken a piece of him with her. She wanted to inflict pain on him and make him suffer as he had made her suffer, but she wasn't brave enough to push through the instinctive envelope of self-preservation. She already knew she was going to pay dearly, but the thought of injuring him and provoking additional rage was unfathomable.

Finally, Frank broke off the kiss.

"Now, are you going to be a good girl?" he asked her in a sugary-sweet voice.

"Yes," she said, her voice trembling, her body braced.

"Okay," he said with a knowing smile. "We are going to have some fun tonight. I'm going to go easy on you, so relax.... Maybe you'll even enjoy it. Don't worry. Tonight, isn't the night you die. Well ... unless, of course, you don't do exactly what you're told." He said this coyly, as though she were a naughty child.

Bineshiin had absolutely no illusions about what the end result would be; it was just a question of how long she could last. Perhaps she could hope that, if it took long enough, and she behaved, other opportunities for escape would present themselves. She took a deep breath and readied herself.

"Get up, and take off your clothes," he ordered. Bineshiin did as she was told. Then Frank took her by the right wrist and led her to the bed. "Now, get up on the bed, on your hands and knees."

He watched as she crawled up as asked. Bineshiin tried to turn her head and look at Sheldon, but Frank saw her looking and hit her as hard as he could with the paddle.

Bineshiin let out a loud, painful scream. Frank responded by slamming her face down into the mattress, holding her there. She was barely able to breathe as her nose and mouth were buried. Now the real torture started. Frank began to crack the paddle down on her, swift and hard. He would stop in between cracks for a while and watch as her body trembled with terror. He knew that the anticipation of it was worse than the crack itself. She never knew when it was coming or where, or how hard it would be.

"Okay now," he told her, his voice firm, "I want you to get off the bed, bend down, and touch your toes."

Bineshiin complied, dreading what she knew was coming next. As she looked down beside her right foot, she saw the spilled knitting basket on the floor, and right within her reach, a long, steel, knitting needle. She realized that she only had one chance, and that she would have to be quick. Her heartbeat with a flicker of hope.

Stepping up behind her, Frank grabbed her hips and pulled her towards him. He grabbed her braid pulling it towards him so that her face stared up at the ceiling. She braced for what was sure to come next when all of a sudden, he let go of her hair.

Frank's heart stopped in its chest, his lungs burning and his stomach lurching wildly. He saw her. There she was. His Lucy. Rotten, with one eyeball hanging down out of its socket onto her cheek. He could smell damp, musty earth, and the pungent odour of rotten leaves. She walked toward him slowly, one long finger raised and pointing at him.

Sheldon was floating somewhere between consciousness and unconsciousness when the smell of roses suddenly overwhelmed him. He breathed in deeply and saw a little blonde girl, propped up on pillows in her bed, knitting a yellow blanket. She would stop once in a while and feel her belly. She stopped what she was doing then and looked at him with eyes so much like his own that he felt as though he were looking into a mirror. She smiled lovingly at him and motioned towards the stairs. He understood. Climbing to

his feet, he hurried up the stairs and grabbed the shotgun from the wall.

Bineshiin heard the sound of the paddle dropping from Frank's hand to the floor and braved a look at him, preparing herself for his next act of madness. But when she looked back, she saw that his face was dead white, and his wide eyes were staring blankly forward into the abyss.... He was muttering and mumbling incoherencies, completely lost in some sort of trance.

She didn't waste any time. She grabbed the knitting needle, turned around quickly, and punched it into his stomach. He backed up in disbelief. He looked down at his stomach watching the blood spilling over his hands. Bineshiin ran towards the stairs and saw Sheldon descending with the shotgun.

Frank fell to his knees. "Sheldon ... please.... Please help me," he begged. Sheldon put the weapon to his shoulder but found himself still unable to pull the trigger.

After a frustrated moment, Sheldon lowered the weapon, and they both turned and ran, leaving Frank bleeding in the basement alone. At the top of the stairs, Sheldon picked up the phone and dialed 911. He was yelling his address to the operator, when he heard his father trudging up the steps. He dropped the phone, grabbed Bineshiin and they ran. They slammed into the front door, which was firmly locked and dead bolted. Panicked, Sheldon fumbled with the locks, trying to open the door.

"Hurry, Sheldon!" Bineshiin screamed. "HURRY!!"

Finally, the locks gave way, and Sheldon fell outside onto the front step, Bineshiin tumbling after him. As Sheldon got out from under her, he grabbed her hand to help her to her feet. He was unable to pull her to standing because she was being dragged backwards by Frank. She started screaming and kicking at him, but stomach wound aside, he could still overpower her.

Sheldon charged toward him, rifle at the ready, but just before he reached the door, he felt a rush of wind pass above him towards the house—towards his father in the doorway.

Sheldon stopped and watched as an eagle attacked his father, screeching and scratching. Terrified, Frank released Bineshiin and scrambled past her out the door. The bird swooped in on him repeatedly, knocking him down onto the snow and ripping at his face and body with its giant talons.

Finally, the bird backed off, and hopped towards Bineshiin, settling beside her on the steps. It gave a strange whistling croak, flapping its wings, and then as Sheldon watched, it cocked its head towards Frank, who was still trying to get up.

Bloodied, battered, and pulsing with rage, Frank made one last run at Bineshiin.

The sound of a shotgun pierced the night air as Sheldon pulled the trigger—the same trigger that he had fantasized about pulling every night of his life. And at the same target. He looked down at his Father then with no feeling whatsoever as he watched the blood drain from what was left of his head.

Bineshiin ran to him and collapsed in his arms. They stood

that way forever, even when they heard the whoop of police sirens ripping up the dirt road. As they held each other, they both looked up to see the moon resting above them, encircled by millions of stars. It was enough to take their breath away. As they watched, they saw the eagle circle above them once more before settling down onto a nearby tree branch and looking at them intently.

"Bineshiin ... that eagle is here for you. It was with you the night I found you," he said, barely believing his eyes.

Bineshiin stared to look at the eagle; it was magnificently beautiful, and just before it took flight once more, she could swear she saw her mother's eyes looking back at her.

CHAPTER 22

the next day

Sheldon and Bineshiin watched through the glass as Lucy's parents arrived at the station. They both stood up to greet them, and all was silent as they stared at one another.

Lucy's mother looked Sheldon in the eyes. "You have her eyes."

They all began to cry for Lucy and for each other ... to just cry. Afterwards, they spoke for hours, telling each other all that they knew about a beautiful little girl named Lucy. When they stood up to part ways, Lucy's father placed his hand on Sheldon's shoulder and squeezed hard. Sheldon realized that, for the first time ever, he had a family, and a part of his mother as well. Together, they would honour her and keep her memory alive. They exchanged information and they knew that it wouldn't be long before they saw each other again.

Just before they left the station, two police officers were walked past them, both in handcuffs. They scowled at them as they passed. Bineshiin gave them both her largest smile

and watched as they were placed in a room, followed by several men in suits. This was the first time in her life that she had ever been taken seriously. It was sad that it had taken a little white girl's death to make them listen to her, but maybe—just maybe—this experience with her would change their minds just enough to make it easier for those that followed.

The school was finally demolished, and all the negativity that went with it. It was time for a rebirth, to take trauma and abuse and turn it into something beautiful. A geological survey had revealed that there were dozens of children buried around the property, some as young as three years old. Sarah had been keeping the little ones safe in their eternal sleep.

Bineshiin had so many plans, so many ideas, but a lifetime's worth of frustration was still busily churning in her mind. Why did it have to take hundreds of dead children for anyone to listen? For decades, society had turned their noses up to a targeted population. Callously taken away their most basic human rights, their land, their children, and their livelihood. They forced them to the very edges of society, out of their sight and out of their minds.

Even after the children had been found, the Prime Minister couldn't even be bothered to attend the First National Day for Truth and Reconciliation. Yes, the Government threw some money at the situation, but even though the windows

had been blown wide open, it seemed as though society in general, and the Government in particular, barely felt the blast of frigid air. She sighed.

The prejudice, the stigma, and the ignorance will never go away, she thought, *if our own Government keeps turning a blind eye and covering the windows with rose-coloured curtains.*

Sheldon and Bineshiin recognized what that they were up against. It was a battle of many, stuck outside the front gates. Only a few brave souls were able to find a way through; once in, the battle had only just begun. There was no way to take away the egregious acts of their government, but they could join the battle and provide more weapons.

A large memorial was eventually erected where the children had been found, dedicated to all of the survivors and children who had tragically lost their lives at the hands of a government elected to protect them. The burial site was fenced in and "*Every Child Matters*" was emblazoned on each side of the fence. Artists were welcome to come and paint the fence in beautiful, meaningful artwork—her favourite, a soaring eagle. The school grounds were open to the general population to visit and grieve, regardless of their language, religion, or walk of life.

Children visiting the memorial site could put their handprints or write messages on the fence, inside or out. There were benches all around, with stainless-steel plaques that could be engraved to pay tribute to a child lost or survivor that was special to them. There was a cobblestone path running in different directions, and roses grew everywhere,

intertwined with woodland phlox, blood root, and fringed bleeding heart. Wild-flower seeds were provided, and people could throw them anywhere they pleased on the property.

Sheldon, Bineshiin, Larry, and Sheila—even Dino also wanted to help those people who were struggling as they once had with addiction, homelessness, and feeling lost with no way out. They built a large recovery centre where the school had once stood. On-site doctors and nurses would assist anyone who showed up with a medically supervised detox. An educational program was offered, teaching lifestyle skills and behaviour modification techniques. There was free therapy, medical consultation, and treatment. Residents were provided food, clothing, and shelter as well as one-on-one support during their recovery.

Once rehabilitated, they could then move to secondary stages, if they chose to do so, in which they gave back to the community through acts of service: cleaning rooms, gardening, helping others on their path to recovery, and so on.

There was also a nursery for infants and children on site. Arrangements would be made to help struggling parents to continue to hold their children dear, without having to worry about their financial situation. This removed any barriers to care, as the parents had access to their children during their recovery.

Larry and Sheila had sold their motel and built a larger secondary living site on the premises, gently encouraging those in early recovery to succeed by offering them a safe place in which to maintain their sobriety.

Just before the facility opened its doors, Larry, Sheila, Bineshiin, and Sheldon held each other, looking at the sign out front of their long-awaited dream, its large letters over the arch of a rainbow reading "Memengwaa Recovery Centre." The building itself was decorated in butterflies, and it was finally opening its doors to those in need. There were tears of joy, knowing that all the pain and suffering they had lived through had brought them to this point. They were proud, they were alive, and their entire world had come full circle.

It didn't make things okay, of course. None of it ever should have happened to begin with. Still, they had done their best to ensure that Sarah and every other child who had lost their lives were put to rest and memorialized in the way that they had deserved, and that those still in need would have a place to come for help.

Flowers and prayers would never get those beautiful souls the justice they deserve, and there could be no forgiveness for those who had done it, or even knowingly let it happen. But Bineshiin hoped that in some way their recovery centre could help the survivors. If they ended up helping even one person who had suffered the loss of their culture, and their identity, the abuse and addiction in the world—who had endured horrors that most people couldn't even fathom—it would at least be a start to her People beginning to regain the lives that had been stolen from them.

They headed back through the gates towards the centre to prepare for the day's scheduled intakes. Then Sheldon pulled Bineshiin back to him, hugging her from behind and

placing a loving hand on her tummy, caressing their little girl, whose name—they had decided without question—would be Lucy. Sheldon kissed her then and told her he loved her, as he held her tightly. They looked around them once more at the sanctuary they built and knew that no other words were needed. Sarah and Lucy had built this, each in their own way. Their lives would save the lives of many others. Although they'd been little girls when they'd died, their lives had been the trigger for something that Bineshiin and Sheldon hoped would change the lives of hundreds, perhaps thousands, sending a ripple of love and hope to all those who walked through these doors.

As they walked towards the entrance, an eagle soared above them, captivating their hearts and confirming that they had arrived at exactly the place where they were meant to be.

Hearts full, the couple went inside and settled behind the front desk, preparing paperwork for the first set of intakes. The main door gave a little jingle then, and they both looked up. A young woman walked into the room, looking around. Her hair was dark, and her face was pale white, with beautiful patches of darker skin. Bineshiin's heart stopped in her chest.

"Hi," the woman said shyly. "I ... um ... I'm looking for information about my mother."

Bineshiin fingered the necklace at her throat as she stared into the face of Sarah's little lost butterfly, who had finally floated home.

Emily Leigh Curtis lives in Osgoode, Ontario with her husband, three boys and her two dogs. When she is not writing she spends her days quilting and crafting.

Printed in Canada